# Touched by His Vampire Charm

## A Nocturne Falls Universe Story

D1715471

# Kira Nyte

Dear Reader,

Nocturne Falls has become a magical place for so many people, myself included. Over and over I've heard from you that it's a town you'd love to visit and even live in! I can tell you that writing the books is just as much fun for me.

With your enthusiasm for the series in mind – and your many requests for more books – the Nocturne Falls Universe was born. It's a project near and dear to my heart, and one I am very excited about.

I hope these new, guest-authored books will entertain and delight you. And best of all, I hope they allow you to discover some great new authors! (And if you like this book, be sure to check out the rest of the Nocturne Falls Universe offerings.)

For more information about the Nocturne Falls Universe, visit http://kristenpainter.com/sugar-skull-books/

In the meantime, happy reading!
Kristen Painter

# *Thank You*

Thank you to all of my wonderful readers on this amazing journey! A special shout-out to Rebecca Poole for another gorgeous cover, my editor Raina for all of her wisdom and input to make these books the best they can be, and of course, to Kristen Painter for inviting me to take an exciting ride into the heart of Nocturne Falls!

# Touched by His Vampire Charm

The product of an evil scientist's mad quest to create a day-walking vampire, Vivian Hawkins revels in her freedom in Nocturne Falls, a haven for supernatural creatures great and small. The one thing she truly desires is to find a soul mate. Too bad such happiness isn't meant for a monster like her.

Vampire Draven Lourdes chafes under the musty existence forced on him by the Levoire coven. If he didn't need the stuffy old bones to keep his sister safe, he'd leave the coven behind and focus on his adventures. Instead, he has to chase a lead on one of the coven's missing Elders to a small Georgia town— and gets the shock of his life when he meets the sweetest, most beautiful creature he's ever seen.

Vivian is drawn to Draven the instant they meet. Though she knows better, she can't resist the charming vampire's pursuit. It won't last. It can't.

But for Draven, she'll risk anything.

Website for Kira Nyte: www.kiranyte.com
Kira Nyte on Facebook: facebook.com/kiranyte
Kira on Twitter: @kiranyteauthor
Contact Kira Nyte at kiranyteauthor@gmail.com

# Chapter 1

Life was spectacular. Life was a gift.

To Vivian Hawkins, life was a miracle.

Even as she stared down at the splattered smoothie that covered the front of her shirt, dripped off her face, and clotted in her hair.

The customers at her back either snickered or gasped.

Wendy, her co-worker at Magical Mayhem Smoothies and More, rushed to her side with a rag and started wiping her arm. "Geez. We like mayhem, but not done to ourselves."

Vivian giggled as she took the rag and rolled her eyes. "I thought I had that lid on tight enough. I'll get the hang of this in time." She motioned to the customers with the rag. "At least I've managed some extra entertainment for them."

Wendy, a seventeen-year-old "almost senior", as she put it, removed the blender jar from the base and carried it to the sink. "I've got this. Go clean yourself up in the back."

"Thank you."

Vivian wiped her face with the rag as she slipped into the smoothie shop's spacious back room and sighed. Her shirt clung to her, showing off more of her frame than she'd learned most folk deemed appropriate. Glancing toward the office door, she was disappointed to find it closed and most likely locked. Not unexpected. Neither Faunalyn Ayre nor Vivi's brother, Kalen, expected her to work today. The couple had taken off to go hiking outside of Nocturne Falls so Kalen could see what Fawn called "Fall foliage."

She wasn't sure what that meant, but it sounded beautiful.

Hopefully, one day, she'd see the sights her beloved brother was finally living.

Vivian looked around the back room—an organized storage area for equipment, cleaning supplies, and dried goods—searching for something to wear over her ruined shirt. Nothing. Not even an apron.

As she crossed to the large utility sink, she fished her cell phone from her back pocket, unlocked the screen and autodialed Jackson Emery's number.

He picked up on the first ring. "Everything okay? Are you in trouble?"

She laughed. "No, silly. I had an accident."

Jackson grumbled, "Don't tell me you're in competition with your brother's driving record. It's nothing to strive toward."

"Kalen's a good driver."

"He's crashed two cars since you arrived in Nocturne Falls. Two. That's pretty hard to manage."

"The first time, I attacked him. It wasn't his fault," she defended, twisting on the warm water and saturating the rag. "The second time, he was learning how to work that stick thing in the middle of the console."

"That's a shifter, Vivi. For a manual engine. Regardless, are you okay?"

"I need a shirt."

Silence.

Vivian's brows rose as she waited, most of her attention on her efforts to scrub the strawberry smoothie from her white cotton shirt.

"It's just a shirt," she finally added.

"I'm not going to ask why you need a shirt or how yours went missing."

"I'm at Fawn's shop. I wanted to work a little today. I'm wearing a smoothie and I have nothing to change into."

"Ah. Okay. That's better than a car wreck or being shirtless. Your brother would kill me."

Vivian rested the phone on the counter and placed the call on speaker mode to free her hands. She pulled her shirt over her head and shivered as the cold soaked into her damp skin. Thanks to her vampire genes, she wasn't as prone to the effects of the cold, but she didn't care for the chill. Not after her ordeal only a few months ago. That deathly chill always preceded another level of deterioration. But that was before Fawn came into her life.

Vivian owed the nature elf more than her life. Her loyalty to her brother's fiancée and soul mate was unbreakable.

"Any particular shirt? Your closet is overflowing."

"It doesn't matter. Just none of the shirts from Into The Woods. Those are expensive." Vivian sponged her skin down with warm water before unwrapping the band that held her hair back. She leaned over the sink and started washing smoothie from the ends. "I think I have some of those plain T-shirts in one of my drawers."

"Last time I went into your drawers for you, I discovered questionable undergarments."

Vivian laughed. "Women don't wear those boxer things."

"Too much lace. It caught me off guard."

"The shirts are the second drawer down."

As she listened to more of her friend's grousing as he searched, she smiled. She had little self-consciousness in regards to her clothing or her belongings. She'd spent her entire life before Nocturne Falls locked up in a small room at a lab, with as much privacy as your typical lab rat. Modesty wasn't a consideration. Doctors and scientists had seen her naked more times than she could count. She never liked it, but she had no choice. It wasn't until her body started to develop from girl to woman that Kalen put up an argument about his sister being alone with a bunch of male doctors.

He called them Lab Coats. She quietly nicknamed them "monsters." It was fitting, considering the tests and experiments they performed on her and her brother. It was like they had no feelings, had no souls.

She always kept an outward smile for her brother's sake. He hated to see her cry. He hated that he couldn't protect her. She never shared the details of the worst of the experiments with him for fear it would shred Kalen to pieces.

Her beloved brother.

"Okay. I think I found something that doesn't have lace or look like butt floss."

Vivian snorted. "It's comfortable underwear."

"I'll trust you on that. Give me fifteen minutes. I have to change."

"You're still in your pajamas? From *yesterday*?"

"Hey, don't dis the flannel pants. It's getting chilly outside." He snickered. "Besides, I don't have anyone to look good for."

Despite the platonic nature of her living arrangement with Jackson—his uncle helped Vivi and Kalen escape the lab before he was murdered—she knew the young man looked at her with a tad of lust in his eyes. Somehow, he did his best to maintain an almost brother-sister type of relationship with her.

She had to wonder what her older brother had threatened to do to Jackson if he tried to pursue anything more with her after they shared one single little kiss.

It wasn't his fault she had been curious. She saw the pleasure in Kalen and Fawn's faces every time they kissed. Which was a *lot*. Naturally, she had asked Jackson to kiss her so she would know what it was like.

Poor guy had been so flustered. She had to catch him before he fell to the floor.

It didn't matter. Jackson wasn't her soul mate. She had plenty of time to wish and dream and wait for her perfect man to come. She wanted the romance and the love, but she was so new to this world outside of stark walls she had no idea how to go about finding it. She'd bide her time, exploring all the things denied her for twenty-six of her twenty-eight years.

"Thanks, Jackson. I'll see you shortly then," Vivian said, disconnecting the call. She finished smoothing the stickiness from her skin, washed her face, and wrung out her hair. She worked a bit more with her shirt before giving up, leaving a huge pink stain over the front, and squeezed as much liquid from the fabric as she could.

"Uh, would you like me to grab you a shirt?"

Vivian twisted at the waist and stared toward the doorway to the front of the shop. Wendy blinked, a very confused look on her face.

"Jackson's bringing one down for me. Thank you, though."

The young woman's attention darted from Vivian's almost naked torso. It took Vivian a moment to realize her lack of modesty wasn't normal in the real world, though she would have thought the were-panther would have been more blasé about seeing some skin. Maybe what felt comfortable among weres was not acceptable if the other party was not a were-animal of some kind.

She cleared her throat and held her damp shirt against her chest. "I'm sorry. I didn't mean to make you uncomfortable."

"Oh, no. Not a problem. I heard you talking to someone. Wanted to make sure you were okay. Why don't you hang back here until Jackson arrives? There's only a couple of customers in the front. Nothing I can't handle."

"Are you sure?"

Wendy flashed her a genuine smile. "Of course, Viv. No worries at all. You know you can ask me if you ever need something. Jackson isn't the only one who is your friend."

A familiar sting hit Vivian's eyes, one that came so often now, especially with these wonderful people of Nocturne Falls opening their arms and their hearts to her and Kalen. The siblings had suffered so much for so long. Just a speck of kindness drew on Vivian's emotional well.

"I know. Forgive me. I'm still adjusting to much here."

To her surprise, Wendy rushed across the room and wrapped her in a tight embrace. It was short-lived, but the unspoken sincerity in her friendship was as warm as her arms.

"Fawn wouldn't keep me here if she didn't think I was trustworthy. That woman bases her relationships on trust and honesty. I'm your friend. Don't forget that."

As Wendy returned to the front of the store, Vivian sank back to lean against the sink. She hated the emotions that crashed over her at times. It was like she had kept so much bottled up inside her for so long that now, as she experienced true freedom, so did those emotions.

She clenched her teeth and willed away the tears, rolling her eyes to the ceiling. "Get hold of yourself."

She had just enough time to compose herself before Jackson arrived at the front of the store. Wendy took charge of the shirt and brought it back to Vivian, after disclosing their mutual friend's current state of undress. Vivian tugged on the fitted T and secured her hair on top of her head before leaving the storage area. She rounded the counter to give Jackson a hug.

"My savior. Thank you." She pecked him on the cheek and stepped back. "Can I make you a smoothie?"

Jackson blushed. He was a cute guy with permanently mussed dark hair, glasses that constantly slid down his nose, and a wardrobe she determined looked more like sleepwear than outerwear. He shook his head.

"Nah. I'm gonna grab a coffee from The Hallowed Bean and head back home. Trying to reprogram software for a friend in between studying some strands of bacteria."

"Well, good. I'm glad I haven't completely disrupted your day. I'll see you later then."

Jackson waved to Wendy and took his leave.

Yep, normal, everyday conversation between them.

Unfortunately, Vivian knew all too well from snooping around Jackson's lab that those strands of bacteria were actually the remnants of the virus that had nearly destroyed her. Every night, she listened to him mutter to himself about the complexity of the virus and what the worst-case scenario would be if Hugh Ellingham's cure didn't hold.

Vivian took her place behind the counter as a young couple came into the store, arm-in-arm.

"Welcome to Magical Mayhem, where we're more than just smoothies! What can I get started for you today?" Vivian greeted, her smile widening. Why not?

Life was spectacular. Life was a gift. Life was a miracle.

A miracle she felt slipping away into a familiar darkness.

# Chapter 2

"You made it. Finally!"

Draven Lourdes kicked the stand on his Harley and without effort balanced the machine between his legs. He swung his arm, clapping Clark Hamburg's hand and receiving a hard hug and equally hard pat on the back.

"Good to see you, man." Clark straightened up and brushed a hand over his sandy hair. "I was starting to worry you'd learned to abide by the speed limit and wouldn't make it before the fam."

"I'm always point on these ridiculous quests. Like there's any chance the leads the Elders have are anything but nonsense." Draven stretched his arms over his head to ease the tension of the ride from his shoulders and let his hands fall to his thighs dramatically. He cracked his neck with a quick sideways tilt of his head and climbed off his bike. "Sal's been missing for, what? Thirty-five years or something like that? Whatever. It's an excuse to get out of that musty old mansion for a bit. They still think Dracula is a trendsetter."

Clark laughed. "You're kidding, right? Don't tell me they're still all about those flouncy lined coffins and stuff."

Draven pinned him with a deadpan look. He made a circular motion with a finger to his face. "The look of 'I'm not joking.' They think I'm crazy because I sleep in a bed, have a wardrobe that includes some color, ride a Harley, prefer a Corvette, and enjoy going *out*."

"Damn. That sucks."

Draven flashed him a shaded grin that showed off the points of fangs. He grabbed the bag containing his few necessities from the pannier and slung it over his shoulder.

"That means" —

Draven dropped an arm around Clark's shoulders and winked — "you're going to show me all the fun that happens in this little place. I'm livin' it up while I'm in Nocturne Falls."

"In between trying to find out if the rumors that Sal is still alive and being held hostage or that he had kids is true," Clark reminded. Draven snorted and removed his arm from his friend, who continued, "Hey, I've been here for about eight months now and haven't seen anyone or anything that stands out." The guy snickered. "Well, except for the really gorgeous women in town."

Now that was something Draven could only hope for. Being part of the Levoire coven was as drab as drab got. The women were all pasty-skinned, dead-eyed, black-haired tiny things while the men were tall, brooding jerks with no personality. Living in the coven's mansion was like living in a black-and-white movie with no sound.

It was no wonder Salvatore Levoire left and never came back. If Draven were in his shoes, he wouldn't want to lead the coven of walking corpses either. Efforts to push for any change that might move the coven into modern society came up against impenetrable walls. It didn't make the situation of Sal's disappearance any better. He was supposed to take over the coven when Garrett stepped down. He was a spark of hope for those who, like Draven, desperately wanted the family to see what the world was like today. Draven would be long gone from the Levoire coven if it wasn't for his little sister, who was not only allergic to the sun, but had developed a rare allergy to any kind of artificial light. He needed a safe place for her.

Sophia's world was as drab as the coven tried to make it. She had no choice. Everyone else did.

So Draven decided to live for her, to live wild and carefree so he could bring the world to his sister in the form of stories and tales, pictures and trinkets.

That was the bulk of his outwardly carefree existence until he overheard talk about Salvatore's accounts being opened and money withdrawn. After a little more research—according to the Elders, which included Garrett and two other old bones—the coven found that Sal might have left the accounts to children, though it seemed their names were strictly confidential. Those Elders didn't understand identity theft in the current world.

Draven laughed to himself, even now.

*Yeah, right. Sal was the ultimate bachelor. No way did he settle down and have a secret family.*

And that was being respectful. He owed the older vampire everything.

Anyhow, here he was, following a far-fetched lead to a small Georgia town called Nocturne Falls. A place where his friend, whom Draven met on one of his adventures a few decades ago, set down roots because of the many paranormal residents and the freedom to live as who they really were.

Vampires were a *thing*, apparently. Everyone wanted some fang after popular books and movies hit the world.

Draven glanced at this watch. "It's only nine. The night is still young. What do you say I drop my bag off inside and we hit the town?"

"Man, you're gonna love it here!"

Draven tipped his head to the moon, a swollen silver beacon against the star-spangled black backdrop. A few more days, and the moon would be full. He'd be sure to take a picture of it rising behind the trees. Maybe some nighttime pictures of the mountains and the town.

Sophia loved the full moon.

Draven passed up the offer of a short tour of Clark's house. After a few nights of travel, he wanted to get out. His skin itched and it had nothing to do with the chill in the autumn air. He was restless. A few drinks and maybe some darts. He'd prefer a club, but in his experience, midweek wasn't ideal for that in most towns and cities. He doubted it was any different here.

"You say this place is all about supernaturals, right? Any place to pick up some laced wine or, I dunno, a unit or two of A-positive?" Draven asked, settling his tall form in the passenger seat of Clark's Porsche SUV.

"There are a few places." Clark smiled big. "Hope Sophia's prepared for all the little goodies you'll be bringing home with you."

Draven chuckled. "If I discover there is truth to these rumors about Sal having kids, maybe I'll be bringing her *to* the goodies."

Draven glanced at his watch for the tenth time. Forty-five minutes of driving around, listening to Clark's descriptions of places and points of interest that he did care about—"That's the old Piltcher manor, supposedly haunted" and "That's the where the head of Nocturne Falls lives" and "That's Mummy's Diner, with some pancakes to die for"—it took every ounce of control to keep from jumping out of the SUV.

"This is Main Street—"

"Perfect! Let's park and walk."

Draven unfastened his seatbelt and wrapped his

hand around the door handle. Clark rolled his eyes and pulled the SUV into the first available spot. Draven was out of the car and on his feet before the vehicle was parked. He twisted at the waist, stretching his spine, and took a deep breath. A complex mixture of scents pummeled him, making his mouth water and his fangs tingle. All the old bones steered clear of food and drink, unless is was the thick red stuff, but he loved a rare steak, beer, and even ice cream.

Right now, whatever the delicious aromas were that filled his lungs, he wanted. Bad.

He looked up and down the street as Clark locked up the SUV and met him on the sidewalk. His brow quirked at the throngs of humans weaving about the sidewalks, streaming in and out of stores. He caught bits and pieces of excited conversation. He snickered at the sight of costumes.

"Halloween is still a few days away," Draven said. Perhaps a little too loudly. A group of young ladies dressed as fairies with glitter makeup and teased hair shot him a questioning look.

One blushed and smiled.

He winked.

"It's always Halloween here." Clark knocked him in the shoulder. "Stop it. Don't mess with the mortals. Damn, you're like a caged dog on the free and clear after years on a leash."

"Decades, my friend. Many decades." Draven shrugged, peeling his focused attention away from the women and back to Clark. "Where to eat?"

"Right there, buddy." Clark motioned to a building with Howler's Bar and Grill on the sign. He brushed by Draven to lead the way. "C'mon. You're gonna love the grub. Some of the best bar food you'll ever have. Then I'll challenge you to a round of darts."

"Now you're talking," Draven said, following Clark as he drank in the stores on Main Street, their unusual architecture, and caught whiff of some supernaturals. Shifters, if his nose was still spot on. "So, what types of…things…are here?"

Clark grabbed the handle of one of the bar's doors and held it open for Draven. "You name it, it's probably here."

Stepping Howler's was evidence enough that Clark wasn't exaggerating. Shifters, witches, a vampire or two, humans. Draven smelled and saw and had to keep his jaw from crashing to the floor.

He had never imagined a place like this existing in the world.

"Looking for a roommate? I think I might move in with you," Draven said, his voice vaguely awe-stricken. He shook off his amazement in time to see Clark dropping down into a booth. Draven took up the opposite seat and leaned over the table. "And the humans don't realize that they're walking among predators?"

"Couple of rules, eager beaver. No attacking, feeding on, or messing with mortals. They have no clue that we're real. The bottled water they drink has some kind of spell attached to it that causes humans not to realize what they're seeing isn't more than a show. A nice trick for a bit of freedom, right?"

"Crazy," Draven murmured, panning the bar with a slow glance. "I thought the sign coming into town was a sales gimmick."

"Nope. Every day *is* Halloween here in good ol' Nocturne Falls."

"Wow." *Wolves, panthers, bears. Oh, wait, did that woman just spell some light over her fingertips? And what the heck is that big, burly guy?* He couldn't get a solid scent, but the male was pretty damn stone-faced. His eyes narrowed. "Don't tell me that's a"—he lowered his voice to a whisper—"*gargoyle.*"

"I won't, but he is."

Draven shook his head and turned back to Clark. "What about dragons?"

"Yup. There were a few, as I understand it."

"Pixies? Brownies?"

"Chocolate fudge, caramel filled—"

"Stop."

They laughed as a server approached. He dropped some menus on the table. "What can I get you to drink?"

"Two IPA bottles and two orders of your bacon cheeseburgers. The half-pounders, rare, with all the trimmings sans onions, and an extra side of beer-battered chicken fingers," Clark ordered.

"That'll be all?" The guy looked at Draven.

"Well, I guess I'm having a cheeseburger and…chicken?" His lips curled back. "Do I look like a guy who eats chicken, Clark?"

Clark made a dismissive motion with his hand. "That'll be all. Thanks." His smile grew as the server picked up the menus and left. "I hate chicken, but these things are ingenious."

"Next you'll tell me dressed-up greens are delicious." The corner of his friend's mouth twitched. "Oh no."

"It's really not bad, with good dressing."

Draven ran a hand down his face and groaned. After a long moment, he dared to meet his friend's gaze, only to find Clark's amused expression. Thankfully, their beers arrived a short time later and Draven took a hearty drink after ordering a backup.

"So, tell me why Garrett thinks Sal might be coming out of the woodwork," Clark said.

"There's been quite a bit of activity on accounts that have been untouched for decades. Not much money being taken out, but it's triggered curiosity. When Garrett asked some of his outside sources to follow up on the activity, they were able to find that if it is Sal, he changed his name to Kalen Hawkins." Draven took another guzzle of beer. "But, you know, if Garrett would shake hands with modern times, he might have asked to get some sort of video surveillance or something to show us if it is Sal or not."

"Do *you* think it's him?"

Draven almost snorted his next drink of beer out his nose. Somehow, he managed to get it down his throat. "Salvatore Levoire would not change his name for any reason. That guy was proud of who he was."

When the server came back with his second beer and their food, Draven grew quiet until he was alone once more with Clark. Keeping his voice hushed, he added, "I have a feeling Sal was sabotaged, kept under wraps. If he's still alive, I think we'll find him with this Kalen guy."

"Then the guy isn't human. If he's able to keep Sal contained, he's a strong creature. Unless he got Sal on an off day with some hefty tranquilizers or something."

Draven was almost distracted by the delicious aroma wafting up from the burger. He lifted the bun and poked at the meat. Red juice ran out of the steaming hunk of goodness.

"I'm not sure what I don't like more. That Sal could have been bested by someone of lesser strength with drugs or that someone knew who and what Sal was and had the power to defeat him. But why keep him prisoner for decades and then, out of nowhere, start milking his accounts? Why not do it years ago? It wouldn't have raised suspicion, at least not as strongly."

"You said not much is being withdrawn. Why would that be? Last I understood, Sal's accounts were pretty healthy."

That was an understatement. Sal was the wealthiest member of the Levoire family, next to Garrett. He had access to funds Draven—part of a gypsy family of vampires Sal had convinced Garrett to take into the coven—could only dream of. Draven might not have the infinite wealth of the born Levoires, but he had earned himself a nice savings that, had he been mortal, would allow him to live extremely comfortably for the rest of his days.

Draven had no answer for Clark. It was only a niggling feeling that perhaps speculation about Sal having sired offspring might be rooted in a seed of truth.

The question remained: Where was Salvatore Levoire? And who was Kalen Hawkins?

"Where do you plan on starting? And what links Sal to Nocturne Falls?" Clark asked, dabbing a chicken finger into some yellowish sauce. "The only bank in town is Nocturne Falls Credit Union, and I'd venture to say he doesn't have an account with them. They're not national or international. They're only here."

"Debit card transactions are all linked to this town."

Clark's brow lifted and he stopped dunking the chicken. "Here? Where here?"

"I think a few of the places are Illusions, Enchanted Garden, The Hallowed Bean, Into The Woods. A few restaurants, I believe. I'll start investigating tomorrow evening. Sun sets early this time of year, thankfully. It'll give me a little more time to prod before places close."

"A great chance to get to know the town a bit more."

They finished up their meals and beers, played a few rounds of darts—Draven was chagrined to realize he needed to brush up on his skills—paid the tab, and left. Draven held the door for another couple coming out behind them. When he turned to follow Clark, he bumped into a woman, who stumbled a step before catching her balance. Her friend, a pretty golden-haired woman with lavender and gold eyes, cast Draven a pointed look.

"Excuse you," the woman said.

Draven barely noticed her reprimand as his eyes fixed on the gorgeous creature with hair so pale a blond it could easily pass as white and eyes so crystal clear and blue he thought he was looking into a shallow pool of ocean water. Or ice. But they weren't cold. Not at all.

The two women continued into the bar. He didn't miss the lavender-eyed one's muttered, "Lost his tongue. Can't even apologize. What a jerk."

"Draven, you coming? Or should I pick your jaw up off the ground?"

Draven cleared the knot from his throat and tried to will down other parts of his body.

Oh, but that magnificent creature—she was far from a woman, too much of a goddess—cast him a shy glance over her slender shoulder before letting her friend led her into the bar he had just left.

He had the urge to go back for another round of drinks and more chicken fingers.

Clark scowled. "Man, do I need to teach you common courtesy? You could've apologized. Great way to make a good first impression. And to Fawn Ayre, of all people." Draven rubbed the back of his neck, confused by the surge of sensations and tumultuous emotions that struck him like a truck straight into his belly and chest. "Drave?"

21

"Yeah, okay. I was…" He tried to clear the sandy grit from his throat. "I was a bit stunned. Which one was Fawn?"

"The blonde."

"They were both blond."

"The golden blonde, then."

"And the other?"

When Clark didn't answer, Draven turned a dour look on him. His friend shrugged.

"She's new to town. Only a couple months or so, but no one really knows much about her. I gather Fawn is protective of her."

"What do you know about her?"

"I understand she might work a few shifts at Fawn's shop. It's a smoothie place down the road. We can check it out tomorrow."

Draven took a single step toward Clark before throwing up his finger. "Hold on."

"Drave, what are you…*seriously*?"

Draven yanked open the doors, strode into the bar and scanned the crowd. It didn't take long to spot the pale-haired goddess tucked in a booth, laughing with the female bartender and the golden-haired woman.

Only now, he caught the pointed ears of both fair-haired ladies. Fae? Elves? What else was in this town?

Before he lost his gall and his mouth turned to desert sand, he bee-lined straight to the table.

All three ladies grew silent and looked at him. The bartender—he scented werewolf—arched a brow over golden eyes. The golden-haired fairy-elf-creature with tight lips and a flare of disinterest in her eyes frowned. The goddess…

She melted him with a look brimming with curiosity, innocence, wisdom, and timid reserve.

"Did you forget something, sir?" the bartender asked.

"Uh, no. Actually, I wanted to apologize to your guests. I bumped into this lovely woman"—he motioned to the blue-eyed beauty—"and I couldn't find my voice to say sorry. I was, well, I guess you could say taken by…you."

*Smooooooth operator.*

He mentally smacked the back of his head, followed by a swift kick to his butt. He sounded like an idiot.

The bartender snickered. "You don't come across too many like this." She hitched her thumb at Draven. He wasn't sure whether it was an insult or a compliment. "At least he has the guts to apologize."

"Must've overheard me call him a jerk."

"It's okay," the goddess said. "Really. It was an accident. I saw you holding the door for that couple."

Draven braced a hand on the back of the booth to hide the sudden tremor of his knees. The woman had a voice so soft and calm, so beautifully serene, that he wanted to fall into the seat beside her and listen to her speak for the rest of the night.

*What on Earth is wrong with you, man?*

Some part of his body or mind had to know. Consciously, he was clueless, but anatomically, he responded with a bit too much eagerness.

He held out his hand. "Draven Lourdes. I just arrived here a few hours ago."

"Vivian—"

"Hey, sorry I'm late."

A weighted ball dropped from Draven's chest to his gut. The woman, Vivian, had started to reach out her hand to take his, but dropped it on the table as her attention diverted from him. He glanced from her as a tall woman with brown hair highlighted with hues of dark blue slid into the booth beside the woman Clark had identified as Fawn.

She smelled wolfish, and the gleam in her sharp eyes when she looked at him, confirmed it.

"Who's this?" the new guest asked.

"I was just about to leave." He looked at Vivian, pleased to find her attention back on him, accompanied by a soft blush over her cheeks. "I hope to see you again."

Vivian graced him with a smile as he walked away. He paused at the door of the joint long enough to toss her a lingering glance and half-grin before leaving for the second time.

"Well, I sure hope you didn't make a bigger fool of yourself," Clark said, pushing off the brick wall next to the door.

Draven shrugged, ignoring his friend's burning gaze. "Guess we'll find out soon enough."

# Chapter 3

Licks of icy cold shadows caressed her mind, but she mentally swatted them away.

For over a week, this precarious dance with darkness haunted her. Freedom was becoming a battle, one she did not want to fight, but one she would not lose.

Vivian curled her fingers against the counter and closed her eyes. The sweet and delicious scents of Magical Mayhem faded as the darkness fought to latch onto her consciousness.

She pressed her lips together, a familiar lump forming at the base of her throat.

*Don't make me fight this again. Please.*

Like evil ever listened to reason. Or the pleas of an innocent host.

"Vivi, is everything okay?"

Vivian opened her eyes as she forced her fingers to relax and a smile curled her lips. Kalen leaned against the doorway to the back of the store, his eyes narrowed on her and his arms crossed over his chest. Suspicion darkened his eyes and sharpened his handsome features.

Her beloved brother. She could not bear putting him through the anguish and pain of watching her slowly go crazy beneath the spell of the poisonous serum. The last experiment performed on her would have killed her had it not been for Kalen's determination to cure her.

"I thought you'd be long gone by now." Vivian cast her eyes towards the front of the store. It was unusually quiet, even for the late hour. The crowds on the sidewalk beyond the windows had thinned as evening turned to night. She'd be closing up the shop in about a half hour. She hadn't even heard Kalen come in, another unsettling hint that Hugh Ellingham's cure hadn't cured her, simply masked the evil for a few months. "It's late and I'm sure Fawn is waiting for you."

"I stopped by to pick up some paperwork she left here earlier." He rustled the folder tucked under his arm. She had missed it on first look. "You look pale."

She laughed and waved his concern aside. "So do you, if we're going to talk skin tone."

"Vivian."

She forced her smile to widen as she stepped up to him and kissed him on the cheek. "Don't take that tone with me, big brother. You have another woman in your life now. Your focus should be on Fawn."

"My focus is on you both."

"I'm a big girl." She touched his shoulder. "There are times I reminisce, that's all. Just...sordid memories."

The sternness in his expression softened, but his brows furrowed with growing concern. He caressed her hair and sighed. "You would tell me if something is wrong?"

"Of course." The lie practically choked her, but she couldn't tell him otherwise. "Now go. I'm trying to clean up so I can save Jackson from becoming one with his computer screen."

"No other...incidents have occurred between you two, have they?"

Vivian snickered and shook her head as she turned away. "I told you, it was just an innocent kiss. I don't think of Jackson that way."

Kalen grunted.

"Brother, what are you going to do the day I find a man who kisses me the way you kiss Fawn?"

Kalen groaned and pushed off the doorframe without answering. "You'll be okay closing up? I can stay and help."

"Go, Kalen." She pointed toward the back door. "I love you to the ends of the universe. Now go."

Kalen chuckled and shook his head. He brushed a kiss on her forehead before he disappeared out the back door. Only once she was certain he was gone did she let her shoulders sag. She wasn't sure what was worse. Lying to her brother about what was happening to her or facing the monster alone. She hadn't confided in Jackson, either.

Vivian loaded her arms with pans of fruit and granola and brought them to the walk-in fridge in the back room.

When she returned to the front, she came up short. The corners of her mouth twitched with the onset of a natural smile and her heart did the same silly flutter it performed the night before.

Draven Lourdes, a masterpiece of sharp-edged handsomeness softened by a charming smile and twinkling blue eyes, stood at the counter by the register, resting a hip casually against the edge. He had a thumb hooked in his black leather belt and the other hand tucked under his arm.

Vivian tried to take a breath, but it jammed somewhere between her nose and her throat. Good thing her vampire genes didn't need oxygen and her fae genes needed little. Those gorgeous blue eyes moved over her slowly, and she felt every inch of that perusal as if it were a physical touch.

Her skin tingled and warmed.

The darkness inside her vanished, almost as if it feared the man standing a few feet away.

"I didn't mean to startle you." His voice was deep and husky, sexy and fluid. Black hair hung over his forehead, the ends brushing his pale cheeks. He pressed off the counter and arched a brow. "I hope I'm not interrupting something."

Vivian cleared her throat and laughed nervously,

lowering her head as unnatural heat burned her cheeks. She chewed her lower lip for a moment before mustering enough strength to meet Draven's watchful gaze.

"I'm sorry. No, you're not interrupting anything. I was just cleaning up for the night." She motioned to the cooler with a trembling hand. Wow, her nerves were overset. Her entire body was overset, from the persistent fluttering of her heart in her chest to the pleasant turn of her belly. "Can I get you something?"

The corner of his mouth curled into a devilish grin. "Actually, I was hoping you might be available for a drink."

Vivian stared at him, flabbergasted. A drink? Was he asking her on a…date?

"I, uh, I…" A drink with Draven. The more she looked at him, the harder she found it to look away. "How did you know where to find me?"

Draven waved toward the front door. "My friend suspected you might work here. I figured I'd give it a shot. I want to make up for my poor manners from last night."

"You *had* apologized." Vivian busied herself gathering another section of pans from the display cooler. She stole several glances at Draven while she covered the pans with plastic wrap. "I believe you'd be outdoing yourself with a drink."

Draven moved with a fluid grace that reminded her of Kalen as he stepped in front of her on the opposite side of the display. He folded his leather jacket-clad arms over the top of the curved glass.

"So, you accept my invitation," he assumed.

"What"—she pulled plastic wrap over another pan—"makes you believe that?"

"The way you're hiding your smile."

Vivian blinked and looked up at him. She was shocked when he reached out and brushed a finger over her cheek. Not from the motion, necessarily, but the string of hot tingles that followed the path of his simple touch.

"Don't hide it. It's too beautiful to be stifled." He replaced his arm on the top of the case. "Allow me to make up for my fumble."

She wasn't sure she understood what he meant by fumble, but she had made up her mind. There was a strange magnetic pull to the man, one she couldn't shake. One that kept her up all night and all day with visions of Draven's winning smile and blue eyes consuming her mind.

Vivian rested her hands flat against the narrow counter behind the display and lifted a brow. "One drink."

Draven pursed his lips in thought and gave a slow nod. "And what if I win your attention for a second?"

She laughed and piled the covered pans on top of each other. "Excuse me. I'll be right back."

"Can I be of assistance?"

"You can greet anyone who might come into the store while I'm putting these away."

Vivian cast him one last glance before turning toward the back. The grin he wore paired with the intrigued gleam in his eyes was devastating in the best way. His gaze lingered on her until she disappeared into the walk-in.

She had never been more thankful for the blast of cold air that cascaded over her skin, soothing the burn that had taken up residence since Draven's arrival. She stored the pans in their designated places and took a deep breath to calm her nerves before returning to the front.

Draven lounged against the side of the drink cooler, cell phone in hand, fingers texting at a rapid pace. Too rapid for a human, not that she suspected he *was* human. She narrowed her eyes, utterly aware of the smile growing on his mouth.

"Sorry. My friend was asking when I'd be home," Draven explained, locking the phone and tucking it in his jacket pocket.

"You seem a man who would enjoy the sunlight," Vivian ventured to guess. Draven's smile waned only a smidgen, but his eyes grew sharp. "But you can't, can you?"

"I was under the impression speaking of our origins in public domains was taboo." He pointed to the sign hanging in the door's window. "Should I flip it to Closed?"

Vivian glanced at her watch and nodded. "If you don't mind. And turn the bolt lock, please?"

Draven did as she asked while she pulled the last of the pans from the display and returned them to the walk-in.

"I'll tell you mine if you tell me yours."

Vivian spun around, her shoes slipping on the tiled floor of the walk-in. He caught her under the elbow and steadied her. Damn him for knocking her emotions so off-kilter that her own heightened senses failed to pick up his presence.

"You shouldn't be back here," she said, easing her elbow from his hand. "For employees only."

Draven sighed. "My apologies. This is uncharacteristic of me." He stepped back, giving her room. His gaze stayed on her as the silence stretched. His grin was gone and his expression filled her with a startling swell of indescribable heat. She was beginning to wonder if this was what happened when Kalen met Fawn. Draven cleared his throat. "I'll, uh, wait in the front."

"Vampire, are you?" Vivian said quietly, catching him mid-turn. He twisted back and watched her carefully. She shrugged. "Your grace when you move is hard to discount. Men your size shouldn't be able to move like ghosts."

"I'll accept that as a compliment." His grin returned, and so did the flutter in her chest. "I'm uncertain as to you, though." He began to reach toward her head, and her ear, she suspected, but caught himself and lowered his arm. "I don't mean that in any negative form."

This flirting routine was new to her, but she had watched enough romance movies while locked away in her small room at the lab that she had an idea of how to play the game. She'd give it a try.

She stepped up to him, pressed up on her toes, and whispered in his rounded ear, "Fae."

Then she sidled by him, out of the walk-in and returned to the front of the store. She wasn't ready to confide she was more than fae. Jackson's uncle, Nicholas Tennerston—who had died helping Kalen and her escape the lab—had suggested they keep the vampire half of their heritage secret. It was easier to explain away pointed ears than needle-sharp fangs.

"Enchanting."

Vivian glanced over her shoulder as Draven came up behind her. He tucked his hands in his jacket pockets.

"That's the word I was looking for. You're enchanting, and now I understand why."

Vivian let out a breathy laugh. "Aren't you a charmer."

"I'd like to think I'm more of a laidback guy looking for adventure."

"I'm domesticated." She tossed him another glance as she placed lids on the pans that stayed in the cooler and stifled a burst of laughter as his eyes widened. "I'm kidding." She flipped off the lights in the coolers and wiped her hands on her jeans. "I'm going to grab my jacket and purse from the back. I'll meet you outside."

She hesitated in the office until she heard the familiar clunk of the door closing. Quickly, she shot Jackson a text telling him she'd be late, not to wait up for her, and went to meet up with the charming vampire.

If her life were to be stolen from her this time around, at least she would fall victim to the monster having known true attraction.

# Chapter 4

"What is a good place to get a drink around here?"

Vivian walked alongside Draven, their pace lazy and their conversation light. They walked with no destination, despite his invitation to join him for a drink. Every now and again, her arm brushed his, unleashing a flurry of warm tingles throughout her body. She wondered if he felt the same, or if she was simply taken by his looks and charm.

She smiled at his question. "I forgot you only just arrived. And that you...sleep during the day." She motioned down the street to where Black Cat Boulevard intersected with Main Street. When she looked up at Draven—the man was at least Kalen's height, which was a whole head taller than her meager stature—she found his attention narrowed on the gargoyle fountain in the center of the park. "Want to walk over there?"

Draven seemed to shake himself from his thoughts and smiled down at her. "Is that a real gargoyle?"

"I'm not sure. I'm still adjusting to life on the outside."

She clenched her teeth when she realized what slipped from her lips. It earned her a furrowed brow and a hand over hers, pulling her to a stop. She made an attempt to look away and laugh off her loose tongue—how had she been so careless in the first place?—but the blasted man caught her chin with his thumb and forefinger and turned her gaze back to his.

"You don't seem like a criminal who's spent time behind bars," he said, his voice soft, soothing.

A sad grin touched the corners of her lips. "Not in the sense you believe. I wish not to discuss it." She coughed the knot from her throat when he released her chin, but he continued to hold her hand. The comfort she drew from the simple gesture swelled in her chest. "I do know that there is a rotation of gargoyles. Most likely, what you see is real."

"Interesting," he murmured, but she felt his gaze pinned on her, not the fountain.

"We can get a coffee and I can show you the fountain."

"Sure. Coffee is always a good thing."

She nodded. "I agree with that."

And the fact Draven was mentally stacking his questions in his head. She sensed his curiosity grow as they moved toward The Hallowed Bean. His gaze poignant. His voice fluid and deep. His attention piqued.

"These are some pretty cool buildings. I like the ones that look like they're about to crumble into the ground." A hand on her elbow brought her to a stop outside a small seamstress shop and he touched the faux crack in the brick. Succulents dotted the crevice to make it appear as if the building were in massive disrepair and had been for ages. "Spectacular. This town really pulled out all the stops." He tapped the webbed glass in one of the panes. Thankfully, the shop was closed for the night and his curiosity wouldn't call attention to them. "Intentional?"

"Yes. It's a special type of glass. Adds to that worn, haunting feel."

He ran a hand over his hair, but the longer strands fell right back over his eyes. "This place is really interesting. Love the lights. And those brackets on the street lamps are cool."

"The fairy lights add a magical feel to the town at night." She pointed to a magician performing tricks in front of a dense group of onlookers. "There aren't many vendors out tonight, but on the weekends, Main Street is packed with performers. Maybe I can show you around this weekend."

Draven's grin tilted into one of his warm, charming smiles. "Are you implying you'd like another date?"

Vivian paused, a spark of heat touching her cheeks. She laughed quietly, trying to push aside her nervousness. This flirting stuff was all new to her. "Let's see how coffee and the fountain go tonight, shall we?"

Vivian led the way to The Hallowed Bean, soaking up the attractive company. She couldn't help stealing glances at him, taking in his utterly handsome profile. His dark hair fluttered over his forehead in the light fall breeze, the slant of his eyes and brows highlighting the angular cut of his cheekbones and the sharp slope of his nose. Those brief moments when his hand brushed hers, her breath hitched and flutters erupted in her belly.

"Where are you from?" Vivian asked. The would-be lovers in movies always struck up small talk. Couldn't hurt.

"A small mountain town in northwest Maine. Close to the Canadian border. Not much to tell about it. Pretty remote."

"You don't seem like a man who cares for remote towns." He shot her a curious glance. "What I mean is that you seem to have so much life inside you. I'd place you living in a big city."

"That hasn't escaped me. However, as much as I enjoy a populated area, I do look forward to retiring to my quiet little piece of the world." He gave her a playful nudge in the arm. "What about you? I picture you coming from some heavenly realm where you shimmer and glow like stars in the night sky."

Vivian shrugged. He wasn't too far off. She had only recently learned of her Celestial fae roots—the fae who oversee the universe—and the royalty in her blood. Her mother had been from a royal line. She had never met her father, who provided her with the vampire genes. Kalen told stories about him, but their sire had been killed protecting Kalen and their mother while she carried Vivian.

"Maybe I do," she jested half-heartedly. It was far more majestic imagining than the dull gray walls of a room at an undisclosed lab where a mad scientist performed experiments on her and her brother in hopes of creating the perfect vampire. "Maybe I'm from a distant land of twin moons and twin suns, where everything is dripping gold and crystals."

Draven stepped in front of her and faced her. She would have walked right into him had he not grabbed her face between his hands and pressed a kiss to her lips.

The world stopped. Everything around her ceased. The noise. The breeze. The chill in the fall air. She fell into his warm embrace as Draven's lips teased hers. His hands were vampire cool, but almost produced more heat than she could bear. It filtered through her skin and into her veins, burning her up from the inside.

Gods, she had never kissed a man like this. What if she did this wrong? What if she—

His tongue swept through the seam of her lips and into her mouth, slow, gentle. What was hot before dunked her world upside-down into an inferno. She melted with each tender motion as he tested her response to his advance.

She responded with a breathy moan and her arms twined around his neck. She followed his lead, learning this new dance from Draven and loving every moment.

This kiss was nothing like the one she shared with Jackson. Nothing.

Draven tasted like promise and security, two things she desperately wanted in her life. He had no heartbeat, but she could taste the potent strength in the blood beneath his skin. As his kiss grew deeper, so did a primitive hunger that made her gums tingle as her fangs—

"Excuse us."

Vivian tore away from Draven and spun at the sound of the familiar voice pitched low in a feral growl. Sweetness teased her tongue, causing her vision to blur for a brief moment. She dared to glance at Draven. His finger went to his lip, were two small beads of blood glistened. His eyes narrowed on her before she looked away.

Kalen's glare could kill as he stared, unblinking, at Draven. Fawn placed a hand on Kalen's arm in an attempt to calm him.

"It's okay," Vivian said, stepping between Draven and her brother even as Draven moved to protect her. She waved him back and grabbed Kalen's hands until her brother looked down at her. His bright eyes glowed with warning. Even now, months after he believed she was cured and he was engaged and planning to start a life with Fawn, his need to protect his sister ran strong. She cast Fawn a worried glance. "He was taking me for coffee."

"Love, this is the guy I told you about," Fawn added in a tone Vivian knew soothed her brother. The fierce edge to Kalen's face and the sharp cut in his eyes dulled slightly. "The one I suspected had an eye for Vivi."

Fawn took her eyes off Kalen long enough to cast a pointed look at Draven.

"Taking you for coffee and kissing you in the middle of Main Street are two different things," Kalen said. Despite the calm she was certain Fawn was forcing on him with waves of her magic, his voice remained deadly. He lifted his chin enough to ramp up his predatory regard. "Kissing on the first date isn't acceptable."

"Are you her father?" Vivian winced at the challenge in Draven's tone and the worry that crossed Fawn's expression. Vivian saw her grip tighten on Kalen's arm at the same time she stepped back into Draven's chest, forcing him to stand down. "I'm sure she can make decisions for herself."

"Draven—"

"What interest have you in her when you've known her for a matter of minutes?" Kalen took a threatening step forward. Fawn scrambled in front of him and shoved him back.

"Kalen, enough. Your sister can—"

"Kalen?" Draven asked.

*Oh no.*

Vivian didn't like the heaviness that accompanied Draven's inquiry. Realization threaded through that single question. When she shifted to the side enough to look back at Draven, his eyes had hardened, as had his expression—focused on her.

Ice crested her veins and chilled her muscles. She had no idea what was going on, but the man who had taken her in a tender embrace and kissed her until the world disappeared was no longer staring at her.

Instead, she felt like she was looking into the face of a Lab Coat in one of the examination rooms, waiting for the next injection to see if she would survive or die.

# Chapter 5

The shock of feeling the prick in his lips left him reeling long enough to dismiss the threat from the man who interrupted their kiss. The last thing he expected was to taste his own blood on his lips, or to catch what he thought were the red, glistening tips of fangs before Vivian turned away.

He couldn't get in front of Vivian to protect her from the imbecile threatening him, but upon closer inspection, he caught the startling resemblance between the man and the goddess.

Nothing could prepare him for the sucker punch that walloped him below the belt when the golden-haired elf named the other man.

How many Kalens existed in the world? What were the chances of a Kalen coming down the sidewalk to rescue a sister who wasn't in distress?

His *sister*.

Vivian.

He realized as he glared at the woman who was stealing his common sense that he never caught her last name at the bar. She must know of him, who he was and why he was in Nocturne Falls. She must be aware that someone would come looking for the culprits responsible for Sal's disappearance.

"Don't you dare look at her like that," Kalen growled.

Draven ripped his attention from Vivian—best to forget her now—and met the menacing male trying to move around the elf. He gave her credit. She kept step with him.

"Why? Because you know as well as I do that the gig is up?" Draven spat. He pointed to Vivian. "What's your last name?"

The look of dread that came over her face confirmed his suspicions. She knew she was caught.

"Vivi, don't—"

"Hawkins. Why?" Vivian's brows creased. "I don't understand. What's going on?"

Draven scowled. "I can't believe I almost fell for you."

Her eyes widened, the light blue irises filling with shock and hurt. "But…" She turned to Kalen. "What's going on? Do you know him? Is he someone from the lab?"

"No," Kalen said. "But I'm about to—"

"Stop it, Kalen. *Now*." Fawn threw a hand flat against Kalen's chest. Draven watched in utter astonishment as the raging beast inside the man vanished and calm took him over. Fawn spun on a heel and poked Draven in the chest with one painfully sharp fingernail. "Who are you and why the hell do you think it's okay to talk to her like that?"

Draven swiped his tongue across his bottom lip. The lip Vivian's fangs had pierced only moments earlier. He stole a quick glance at Vivian. Her ears. They were certainly pointy like the fae she claimed to be. But he wasn't about to discount the fact he felt fangs.

His brain twisted and spun.

Something didn't make sense.

"Listen, I think we should go somewhere private and talk," Fawn suggested. "There's obviously something happening here, and it's not going to correct itself with fists, cruel words, or accusations."

As hard as Draven tried to remain guarded, her voice calmed him. Calmed him enough to see a shimmer of tears in Vivian's eyes when he looked toward her before she turned her back on him and fell into Kalen's arms. Kalen never took his keen eyes off him, and Draven had to fight the sting of jealousy as he watched the hurt he caused and someone else provide the comfort he wanted to give.

Instead, he turned to Fawn, keeping his face as stoic as possible. "Good idea. Where to?"

The coffee shop or even the smoothie shop would have been decent places to talk.

Instead, Draven found himself sitting stiff-backed and alert in a cute little cottage deep in the forest away from the main part of town.

Kalen clearly had a lead foot on the little sports car's accelerator pedal and had them there in next to no time. Draven wondered whether the guy was intentionally trying to lose him, or even get him killed. Nothing like being immortal and dying in a motorcycle accident after being impaled by a tree branch and burned by the sun. The way his luck was running the last twenty-four hours, he wouldn't want to chance it.

Inside the cottage, Vivian wouldn't so much as look at him. She helped Fawn gather up a tray of cookies and tea in the small kitchen. He was left in the living room sitting across from Kalen in a silence that could unravel a man's nerves. Draven took the time to discreetly take in every nuance of his possible enemy, from the pointed ears to the intense blue and silver eyes. He looked very much like Vivian, except his hair wasn't as pale and his eyes were a few hues darker.

"Kalen, please." Fawn placed a tray on the table between them and raised her brows. "Relax. We'll figure all this out."

Draven tried to get Vivian's attention, but she refused to make anything close to eye contact with him. She went as far as to sit at the opposite end of the sofa from his chair. Fawn sat beside Kalen on the narrow loveseat.

No one touched the cookies or the tea.

"I believe it's safe to ask whether you have any affiliation with Gerald Hamstead, to start things off," Fawn said.

"Who?" Draven was genuinely confused.

"Doctor Hamstead."

Draven shook his head once. "Should I know who that is?"

Fawn exchanged a shuttered glance with Kalen. Vivian curled her legs beneath her on the sofa and rested her head on the arm. It didn't escape him that their set-up was as close to an interrogation panel as one might get in a fairytale cottage. The burning spotlight was on him.

He moistened his lips. Guilt bubbled up inside him the moment he realized back on Main Street that something wasn't adding up. He barely knew Vivian, but he wanted to pull her into his arms and wipe the sadness away, even if she might be responsible for Salvatore's demise. It made no sense. Either he was completely besotted or there were other forces at play.

"He was a scientist who oversaw an illegal lab that has since been shut down," Fawn provided. She was precise with her words, sharing enough information to clarify without giving away everything. She was good at the baiting game.

Draven shrugged. "I'm sorry. You've lost me. I'm no scientist. I deal with real estate investments and stock trading. The coven I come from is pretty, um, old-fashioned."

Kalen's brows lifted slowly.

Draven answered the impending question before the guy had a chance to ask. "Levoire coven. Up in Maine. Sound familiar?"

"Should it?"

"Touché."

"Listen, I think it's safe to say there is some sort of horrible misunderstanding going on," Fawn said quickly, scooting to the edge of the loveseat. Draven saw her fingers tighten on Kalen's knee. The woman had to have impressive power if she could subdue her lover with a simple touch. "You must have Kalen and Vivi confused with someone else."

Draven finally settled back in the chair and shook his head. "No. That's not possible. I'm here to investigate financial activity that traces back to someone named Kalen Hawkins. Charges made in this very town."

He folded his hands under his chin, eyes narrowing on Kalen. In his peripheral vision, he caught the first sign Vivian was paying attention. She lifted her head, but looked at her brother.

"I find it near impossible to believe my coven is searching for a brother-sister team with the last name Hawkins here in Nocturne Falls, and bam. Here you are."

Fawn shot to her feet and stepped in front of Kalen. She spread her arms dramatically. "Okay, hold on, because he's about to lose it." She hitched a thumb toward Kalen. "Lay it out on the table. All of it. Why are you here? What do Vivian and Kalen have to do with you? Why were you so volatile toward them the minute you learned their last name?"

"I'm not the only one who needs to answer questions." Draven jutted his chin toward Kalen. "You don't need to stand between us. I'm sure we can be civil."

Fawn glanced at Kalen, who gave a slight nod.

"You should thank her. She was protecting you, not me," Kalen groused.

Draven chuckled. "I don't need protection from you."

Kalen remained quiet. His confident silence left Draven uneasy. He already knew there was more to the sibling team than met the eye. He'd best tread carefully until he learned more.

To his surprise, it was Vivian who spoke next. "Brother, part of your anger is over the kiss. Let that go. It should not be your concern."

"If he has the gall to disrespect you so vehemently moments after such a *kiss*, I believe it *is* my concern."

"She's a grown woman, Kalen. Let her be," Draven interjected.

Kalen scowled. "You know nothing of her, nor are you privy to that information."

Draven rolled his eyes and stood up.

Kalen appeared in front of him, a ghost whose movement he didn't catch. This time, when his upper lip pulled back in a sneer, Draven didn't miss the pair of glistening fangs.

"Stop it, brother."

Vivian pushed between them, which was a matter of a few inches, and her backside molded against Draven's front. The battle not to react to her nearness was almost impossible to win. She gently pushed Kalen back a few steps.

"Let him speak, and we will, too. I don't believe he's from the lab," Vivian said, her voice soft and soothing. She cast Draven an empty glance before returning to the sofa, but not before Kalen took his seat again. "Neither do you."

"I'm not from a lab. I live in a house," Draven confirmed, sitting down. "A mansion, actually. With the Levoire coven. A very important member of the family went missing a few decades ago without a trace. He was next in succession to take over the coven once the current leader steps down."

"Go on," Fawn urged gently. "Who was this prospective leader?"

"Have you heard of Salvatore Levoire?" Draven asked. The blank stares he received made his dead heart drop. Neither Kalen nor Vivian showed any sign of recognition, and he doubted the fair-haired beauty could lie outright. "Some called him Sal."

"Why would we know this man?" Vivian asked. A faint crease formed between her brows as she looked between Kalen and him.

"His accounts hadn't been touched since he went missing almost forty years ago. Suddenly, over the last two months, they've been active. Here, in Nocturne Falls. Under the name Kalen Hawkins."

The air in the room changed from electric and threatening to heavy and full of dread. Kalen's shoulders grew stiff. If Draven heard correctly, the other man's slow heartbeat ticked up a few beats. The crease between Vivian's brows deepened and her lips separated. She looked more confused than she had a few moments ago.

But Kalen...He knew something.

Draven dug his wallet out of his pocket. He fingered through his credit cards and business cards until he found a folded up photograph of him with Sal shortly before the older vampire's disappearance. He flattened it out and tossed it onto the table.

Vivian leaned over and lifted the photo. She stared at it for a long time before shaking her head and handing it to Kalen. His gaze dropped for a brief moment before shooting up to meet Draven's.

"Who is that, Kalen?" Vivian asked.

Draven arched a questioning brow, leaned his elbows on his knees and folded his hands between them. Kalen's eyes darkened and his skin grew paler.

"Do you know him?" Fawn asked.

Kalen dropped the photo onto the table and cleared his throat. The feral beast of a man cracked, the fight draining from him before Draven's eyes. A sense of shock and vulnerability flooded his expression before he wiped it away with a blink.

"Yes." He pressed his lips together, shot a glance at Vivian and once more met Draven's gaze. "He was our father."

# *Chapter 6*

Vivian snatched the photo off the table and scrutinized the man standing with Draven. Tall, taller than Draven by a couple of inches. Dark hair, light eyes, pale skin. She compared the man's sharp features with Kalen's and with her new knowledge instantly saw the resemblance. The arch of their brows, the hollows of their cheeks. The man in the photo was smiling, fangs shamelessly on display.

Her father. This was the father she'd never met.

"You said he 'was' your father," Draven said. The accusatory edge was no longer there.

"He was killed when I was three. We were... attacked and he protected us so we could escape. Our mother and I. She was pregnant with Vivi. Vivi never met him. I didn't know his name. I only recently learned our mother's name."

Vivian chewed her lower lip as sadness filled her brother's voice. She felt it resonate in the pit of her chest with the ache she felt of never knowing her father. Hating the sacrifice he'd made. Her life was nothing but sacrifice after more sacrifice. Kalen, who almost lost Fawn to protect Vivian. Jackson, who might have been killed because of her. His uncle, who *had* died helping her and Kalen escape the lab. Her parents, to save their children.

It occurred to her the man who stole a kiss that swept her into another world had known her father when she was never given the chance.

Draven was observing her, sympathy in his expression. His eyes were soulful, yearning, calling to her as he took in her reaction. He no longer mentally picked her apart as he had when Kalen and Fawn first showed up on Main Street. The fierceness in his face had disappeared, and softness had taken its place. Regret.

Vivian placed the photo on the table, pressing her lips together against the telltale ache in her jaw. She knew tears all too well. Not something she was proud of, but her life was anything but happy up until a couple of months ago. Even then, there was still despair and anxiety and worry. All of which intensified with the signs of the virus returning to her system.

Fawn clasped one of Kalen's hands and rubbed his knee with her other. Her brother had comfort and support in a way Vivian never experienced. She busied herself pouring a cup of hot tea and stirring in milk and honey. The brooding silence swelled in the room as seconds turned to minutes. It weighed on her shoulders and made her stomach churn. When she lifted the mug to take a sip of the tea, her stomach nearly heaved.

"Excuse me," she murmured, unsteadily returning the mug to the tray with a clatter and standing. Without looking at anyone, Vivian rushed toward the back door.

Fawn's back patio was a serene sanctuary surrounded by her magnificent flowers and plants, but Vivian didn't stop until she reached the forest's edge. She fell back against a tree and stared up into the night sky, her eyes stinging with tears. The cool air bit mercilessly at the moisture as those tears crept down her cheeks. When she sought solace in the light of the moon, clouds cast it in shadows.

"I'm sorry."

Vivian startled at the sound of Draven's voice, swiping the backs of her hands over her face. She sniffled. It was no use hiding her weakened state, but the last thing she wanted from anyone was pity. She pushed off the tree and turned toward Draven. He had his hands jammed in the pockets of his jeans, his eyes lowered to the ground.

"I'm sorry for how I acted earlier. And I'm sorry about your father." Draven sighed. When Vivian finished another rub at her eyes, she looked up and met his sad gaze. "Kalen explained to me that you two only recently were made aware of the accounts Sal left to you. The Levoire family was never aware he had children. Some feared he had been kidnapped or killed because of his place in the coven."

Vivian sucked in a shaky breath. Draven Lourdes. The vampire who kissed her and held her and made her forget.

"How are you related to my father?" she asked, her soul tearing even as the words slipped from her mouth. She may still be learning about the world, but she knew the taboo of relatives and romantic relationships.

"He was a friend. A mentor."

"You said you live in the mansion—"

"Your father convinced the current leader to take my family in. We were a lost group, the four of us. I'm not related to your father by blood, but I learned a tremendous amount from him. He was a wonderful man."

Vivian laughed sharply and shook her head. She raked a hand into her hair and fisted her fingers at her scalp.

"The more I learn, the more lost I feel. Like everyone around me, strangers as they may be, knows me better than I know myself. Do you know how hard it is to learn who you are from other people? Hear stories about those you never knew, and know you would not be here had it not been for them? I remember little of my mother, nothing of my father. Kalen is the only family I know. I learned of my fae roots from Fawn. My vampire roots from Jackson. My entire life consists of puzzle pieces that everyone else has to use to build the picture of who I am."

She really didn't want pity, but as Draven's

expression changed, she realized her small explosion earned her just that.

"Please, Draven." She turned her back to him, surprised by how deep the action ripped through her gut, and leaned once more against the tree. "I want to be alone."

"I understand. I'm around when you're ready to talk."

Goddess, she didn't want to send Draven away, but she couldn't bear the look in his eyes. She needed time to process this new snapshot of her life, her lineage, and she wanted to do it alone.

"Um, before I go, I should let you know that Garrett, the leader of the Levoire coven, will be coming down with two Elders in the next few nights. They sent me ahead of them to investigate before their arrival."

Vivian lowered her head. Why was she getting the sinking feeling that this was going to turn into another rendezvous like the one with Dr. Hamstead and the Lab Coats?

"I'll tell them what I know without revealing your identities. I'm pretty sure they'll be happy to learn of heirs, but with this group, I can't be one-hundred-percent about that."

The longer he hung around, the more Vivian wanted to take back her dismissal. Something about Draven Lourdes soothed her spirit and cast the blackness away.

"Why are you helping us, then? If your loyalties are with this coven?"

"My loyalties were with Sal. I admired him and looked up to him. These others are a joke with their ruffles and breeches and such."

Okay, that got her attention. She twisted enough to catch the humored half-grin on his mouth. It managed to lighten her mood, that grin.

He gave a one-shouldered shrug. "I am grateful that the coven took us in. They've been a tremendous help for my sister, but if I had a choice, I'd go out on my own."

She tilted her head, observing him closely. "Why don't you leave if you're not happy? You have a choice. For that, you should be grateful."

For a long moment, Draven watched her as she returned the favor. She thought she felt his mind trying to peel back the layers of mental protection she'd placed around her secrets.

"You're examining me," she murmured. But his examination was anything but cold and loathsome. She welcomed it.

"I'm trying to figure you out. But I should probably get going, since you want to be alone. I've stayed longer than I should have."

"Wait." She grabbed his hand as he turned to leave. "I was being dramatic. Things this evening upset me." He glanced down at their hands and slowly lifted that deep blue gaze to hers. "Stay."

"Are you sure?"

Vivian nodded. "Yes. Stay. I want to hear about your sister. I feel a sort of…kinship evolving. One that might mirror the relationship between Kalen and I."

Draven smirked. "I admire your brother's protectiveness of you. It does rather remind me of how I am with Sophia." He turned his hand over, catching her fingers in his as they entwined together. Her heart did a little dance. "Well, I guess now would be as good a time as any to get to know each other. What do you say?"

Vivian nodded. "I'd like that."

He kissed her forehead without warning, his lips lingering on her skin like a cool breeze. She closed her eyes and sighed, resting her free hand flat against his chest.

"Good. So would I."

# Chapter 7

The tension in the air had turned to something altogether different. It seemed that whatever transpired between Kalen and Draven before Draven came into the garden after Vivian had eased the threat and turned them friends. Well, maybe not friends. Rather, not active enemies. Peace floated on the air.

"Would anyone like more cookies?" Fawn asked, rising from the loveseat and lifting the empty plate from the tray. Draven wiped his fingertips on a napkin and shook his head.

"I'm good. Those were wonderful, though. Thanks."

"No, love," Kalen said when she looked inquiringly at him.

"Vivi?"

"Do you have any of those chocolate-dipped pretzels from Delaney's?"

Fawn laughed and nodded. "I keep a stash for you. I don't think I took them out of my bag yet."

Vivian climbed to her feet and eased out between the table and Draven's knees. His hands barely touched her knees to guide her, but he might as well have wrapped her up in his arms and set her on fire, for all that little touch did. Fawn's eyes widened slightly and a secretive smile came to her mouth. Vivian's cheeks warmed when she finally came free of the sitting area.

She cleared her throat, letting her hair hide her cheeks. "Where are they? I'll grab them."

"In the bedroom." Fawn put the plate on the counter. "Follow me."

Vivian knew what that meant. Fawn didn't have to show her where the bedroom was. The two men began talking, discussing what the Levoire coven's mansion was like. Kalen skillfully dodged any questions about where they had been for decades and who their mother was.

Fawn closed the door to the bedroom.

*Oh, that look.*

She was about to get interrogated.

"So, you're chumming up to him?" Fawn kept her voice hushed. She grabbed Vivian by the hands and pulled her down to sit on the bed. "I can't believe I saw you two kissing. *Kissing.* He must've really swept you off your feet for you to fall that quickly."

Vivian giggled, rubbing her cheek self-consciously against her shoulder. "I haven't fallen for him."

Fawn dipped her head. "Yeah. Sure."

"I haven't. How could I? He bumped into me last

night and came to the shop tonight right before closing. I hardly know him."

"You were kissing him, Vivi. You don't kiss guys at random. And you certainly have never kissed a guy the way you were kissing Draven. That was *the* kiss."

Vivian quirked a brow. "*The* kiss? I'm not sure I understand."

"Oh, girl, you know exactly what I mean. That was the kiss of instant attraction. The kiss that sucks you in until you lose all control of yourself and you can think of nothing other than him." Fawn's fingers tightened around Vivian's hands. That mischievous smile widened over her mouth. "And I've been watching him. The way he looks at you. The way he is concerned about your reaction to what he says. He's pretty in tune with you for a stranger. Definitely a charmer."

Vivian knew there was more to Fawn's disclosure than she said out loud. There was an implication lying silent until Vivian realized exactly what Fawn was getting at.

She sucked in a sharp breath. "You don't think…?"

Fawn shrugged. "Full moon is only a couple of nights away. Why not see? It's obvious there is something strong between you two. I can sense it. Your brother senses it, even though he won't admit it because he's gotta be all protective big brother. Kalen would've torn Draven apart if he didn't think there was something deeper going on, and you know it."

Yes, Draven would be missing some pieces and parts, she was certain.

Vivian leaned close to Fawn and said barely louder than a whisper, "What if he can't accept me? For what I am? For everything I've been through?" She lowered her eyes. "What if something goes wrong and I turn back into the monster?"

"Vivian, you've been cured. You've got nothing to worry about. But if something happens again, we'll stand by you like we did the last time."

Vivian mustered a smile. Kalen and Fawn would never abandon her. She would be a fool to discount their loyalty. But Draven. What about him? She barely knew the man, but Fawn was right. There was something between them. Something strong and powerful, promising.

He infused a potent hope inside her when she needed it most. He also made her aware she couldn't delay paying Hugh Ellingham a visit any longer.

If she had any hope of finding the happiness she saw in her brother's eyes and heard in Fawn's voice, she needed to permanently banish the monster slowly growing strength inside her head.

It didn't take a genius to see the path the conversation went anytime Draven attempted to learn more about the Hawkins siblings. He had to give Kalen credit for his smooth side-glances into answers that gave him no more insight than he had before he came to Nocturne Falls. The man may not have much information about Sal, but he certainly had secrets he wasn't willing to give up.

Guess he'd do the same, if his secrets were that dark.

Which made Draven wonder about Vivian and her secrets. Was the woman as innocent as he believed? As he felt in his bones? He'd never been led astray, having always trusted his keen instincts. Those same instincts that wouldn't let his mind free of the grip the woman had over his thoughts, or the conflict she left in his heart.

He dared not listen in on the whispers between the two women in the bedroom. He *tried* not to. Honest. And he didn't, really, until he heard them mention the full moon and finding out something.

"What line of fae did you say your mother was from?" Draven asked, taking a sip of a fresh cup of coffee. Kalen flicked him a glance as he finished stirring honey into his tea.

"I didn't." He took his mug and settled back in the sofa. His body language spoke of his comfort with Draven, although the faint lines of tension along his neck warned him otherwise. "Is your sister older than you?"

Another smooth bunt.

Draven shook his head. "Younger. By twenty-three years. But in terms of vampire lifespans, that's probably equal to the age difference between you and Vivian."

"What is your age?"

"One-hundred and eighteen. Came about at the turn of the century." He hitched his thumb to motion back. "Last century."

The corner of Kalen's mouth curled. "I'm pretty good when it comes to math."

Draven straightened. "I didn't mean it to be taken—"

"I know," Kalen interrupted, lifting a hand to silence Draven. "What are your intentions toward my sister?"

Well, he should have expected the question at some point, but he had been so caught up trying to figure out more about Kalen and Vivian, he had forgotten.

"Because I don't agree with a man she barely knows taking advantage of her."

Draven nearly choked. Kalen kept his gaze steady as he sipped his tea, watching Draven like a hawk. It had been a very, very long time since anyone could make him feel as small and vulnerable as a mouse.

"I would never take advantage of any woman. Especially Vivian. I can't give you an answer as to what came over me earlier, but that was very unlike me. I swear. I didn't mean any harm by it." *Babbling fool.* Draven wiped a hand over his chin and groaned. "I like her. I want to get to know her. There's something in her eyes that draws me in. Something in her smile that…"

Draven cleared his throat when he remembered who he was rambling to. Kalen's slowly arching brow succeeded in making his cheeks warm. Something that *never* happened to him. Until last night.

Damn.

"A date," Draven said, his voice scratchy. "I was taking her on a date tonight."

"Don't hurt her, you hear? She's been hurt enough."

Draven never imagined those words crashing down on his shoulders with the weight of the universe. He never imaged he'd see Kalen as anything but a fiercely loyal and protective brother.

No. Something in the man's face cracked. Something in his eyes shattered. The air in the room turned painfully sad. He wondered who had hurt Vivian. Had it been this Dr. Hamstead they mentioned earlier? Well, one thing was for sure. He wouldn't hurt her if his immortality depended on it.

As if on cue, Fawn emerged from the bedroom, Vivian following behind her. Draven smiled up at her as she approached with a clear bag of chocolate-dipped pretzel rods. She held one out for him.

"They're delicious," she said. "And I usually don't share these."

"She's right. You're lucky she's being kind," Fawn said from the kitchen.

Draven accepted the treat with a smile. "I guess I can't pass up the offer. Not from you."

The blush that touched her cheeks made his stomach flutter. All these strange sensations and emotions that knocked around inside him were as startling as they were comforting.

Her eyes dropped to his knees, which almost touched the coffee table. It jerked him out of his stricken state of mind. He shifted his legs to allow her to pass. She took the seat closest to him and innocently nibbled the chocolate-covered end of her pretzel. His gaze focused on her lips, remembering vividly how they felt when he claimed them. Warm and pliant and full. Oh, he'd love to nibble on them the way she nibbled that pretzel. Maybe he could lick that tiny smear of chocolate from —

The pronounced clearing of a throat snapped his attention away from her. Again. He grappled with his own pretzel as it slipped from his fingers, snatching it a split second after it left his grip.

Fawn, who he hadn't even noticed had rejoined them, snickered. Kalen glowered until she nudged him in the ribs with her elbow. He coughed and forced a grin. Vivian appeared clueless as to the reason for her brother's interruption. Either that, or she hid any reaction behind an innocent expression.

Innocent.

A strange wave of curiosity spread through his mind. Vivian held more wisdom in her eyes than some of the old broods at the Levoire mansion, yet there certainly was an innocence about her.

"It seems the ice has been broken between you two men. My house is still standing and the furniture hasn't been broken," Fawn said. Draven was silently thankful for her smooth attempt to pull his attention from the goddess sitting beside him. He managed a smile and bit into his pretzel. Fawn nodded with an appraising purse of her lips. "No bloodstains. No burn marks from magic. I'm impressed you boys survived some alone time. I was really beginning to worry."

Kalen rolled his eyes and chuckled. Draven was glad to see the man relax enough to relinquish his straight-backed sitting position. He draped his arm around Fawn's shoulders and sank into the sofa, the woman leaning into his side. A sense of yearning hit Draven in the chest when he caught the pure, untainted love they shared when they looked at each other. He took the momentary opportunity to glance at Vivian, who wore a small smile as she watched her brother and his fiancée.

"As long as Draven understands my expectations, I think we'll be well off," Kalen said.

Draven nodded once. He wasn't one to follow directions. He had enough dignity to treat a woman right without guidelines set down by an overprotective brother. Vivian would be no exception to the rule. The only reason he agreed was because he knew he would behave the same way toward a man interested in Sophia.

He understood.

"You'll have nothing to worry about," Draven assured the other man.

"I don't suppose I will."

"Vivian, I would still like to take you out," Draven said. "Maybe tomorrow night?"

Vivian smiled. "I'd like that."

"Great—"

A cell phone buzzed. Vivian dug into her pocket

and put the phone to her ear. The room was silent as she answered with a soft, "Hi."

A chill slipped through the air. Kalen straightened up, his eyes narrowing. A mist dulled Vivian's gaze and her smile fell.

Draven fought the urge to tune into the call until he detected Vivian's heart rate sputter.

"...do everything to fix it. I promise, Vivi. I won't let it hurt you again."

A man. A man who spoke with more conviction than required of someone who was a friend. Draven didn't like it, not a bit, but the sudden heaviness that fell over the room kept him focused on Vivian.

"You're sure?" she asked, her voice weak.

"Come home. I'll tell you more then. Kalen's going to need to hear, too."

Kalen scowled, his fangs bared. "Damn it."

"Oh, well then. Guess I don't have to break the news to him, huh?" the guy asked.

"No. He heard," Vivian said. Her hand and the phone fell to her lap as she disconnected the call.

Draven touched her knee. Her gaze cut to him, shadowed and impossible to read.

"Is everything okay?"

"I, um, need to get home." She stood up, tucked her phone in her pocket, and scooted out from the sofa.

"I know I've got my bike, but I can take you home, if you'd like." He really didn't want to part with her, especially not now, seeing she was obviously not okay. He stood to let her pass, but placed a hand on her shoulder. "No reason for me to stay if you're leaving."

Vivian cast Kalen a glance. He began to wonder if the two had telepathic powers and carried on secret conversations he wasn't privy to.

At last, Vivian lifted her hand to his. He was momentarily shocked by the coldness of her fingertips. "Thank you, but Kalen will bring me home. But, why don't I walk you out?"

Well, guess he settle for the polite dismissal tonight. Tomorrow is a different story. "I'll accept."

# *Chapter 8*

"Hey, Vivi."

Vivian didn't bother looking over her shoulder. She stared out at the brilliant hues of the setting sun from behind darkly tinted sunglasses. Jackson took a seat in the chair beside her on the small patio and handed her a cup of hot tea. She accepted the drink with quiet thanks and placed it on the small table between the chairs without taking a sip.

For a long time, they sat in silence, watching the last of the day drain away behind the trees. Drain away, like the promise of her freedom.

Jackson's phone call the night before delivered the confirmation she dreaded. The truth of her suspicions with evidence from his research. She had known from her increasing sensitivity to sunlight and the flash moments when her mind embraced dark thoughts that went against every grain in her being.

The "cure" Hugh Ellingham provided a few months

earlier was not a cure. It appeared only to have delayed the inevitable. Vivian was beginning to wonder if Dr. Hamstead would end up getting the last laugh, even though he was locked up in jail for life. She wouldn't doubt the beast of a man hoped to destroy both herself and Kalen.

The virus was a sure-fire way of doing that.

"I spoke with Stanhill a little while ago. He's going to fill Hugh in on what's happening, the discoveries I made, and we'll figure this out."

She didn't react. She was numb. She was living a life she had always dreamed of with the promise of happiness oh so close.

Jackson's touch on her wrist drew her out of her thoughts. She slowly looked down at his hand, then followed his arm up to his concerned gaze. His glasses had slid down his nose, but he didn't bother pushing them up. His hair was tousled, strands hanging over his forehead. They did nothing to soften the deep concern in his expression.

Jackson's heart was loyal to both her and her brother. Their pain was his. Failure was not an option. He proved that when she battled the virus the first time, going nights without sleep to sift through years and years of data from his uncle, Nicholas, the man who sacrificed his life to help Kalen and Vivian escape the lab where they lived most of their lives as science experiments.

Dr. Hamstead sought to create the perfect vampire; instead, he created the perfect monster. Vivian had been so close to losing her soul to it that she'd almost killed Kalen. She'd rather die than come that close ever again.

"Have you been feeling it again?" Jackson asked, his voice soft, sympathetic.

"Yes," she answered on a breath.

"For how long?"

"A week now."

Silence stretched until Jackson squeezed her wrist. "Why didn't you say anything to me?"

Vivian shrugged. "Everyone thought I was cured. At first, I wasn't sure if what I was feeling was real or residual effects of my memory."

"You should've said something the moment you thought you felt different. The longer we wait with this thing, the more difficult it becomes to control."

"I was going to go to Hugh and ask him for another shot."

Vivian turned away from the hurt in Jackson's eyes. She confided in him, trusted him. She wanted to keep the monster inside her far away from those she cared about. And since Jackson fell into her inner circle, she included him as among those she cared about. That he continued to research and review the notes and data from his uncle months after her suspected cure bothered her. Too many people had wasted too much time on her.

"You know, Vivi, there is nothing to feel ashamed about. This is not you—"

"That's where you're wrong." Vivian shook her head and stood up, slipping her wrist from Jackson's hand. She met his widened eyes and sighed heavily. "This *is* me. It's a part of me. I don't want it. I don't like it. But it has control over my thoughts when it gets strong. It takes over and I succumb. I can't fight it, so yes. This monster is me."

She sidestepped Jackson's attempt to reach for her hand and went back into the house. She had stayed up all night and all day, contemplating her choices. If she ran away to suffer on her own, Kalen and Fawn would search for her until the end of time. Jackson, too. She debated taking a fake vacation and hiding somewhere far away, but that would only satisfy her loved ones so long before suspicions rose.

"Vivian!" Jackson trotted behind her, moving surprisingly fast for someone who was close to human, and grabbed her arm, forcing her to face him before she could escape to her room. He cupped her cheek with one hand and leveled her gaze to meet his. It took a bit more strength than she wanted to use not to look away.

"*This* is you. Not the virus. That virus will *never* be you."

"Jackson, I appreciate—"

"Stop it. Right now. We will find a cure. A real cure. Hugh's serum worked for months. It'll work again and during that time, we'll work that much harder to figure things out. Vivi, please. Don't lose hope now."

A knock on the front door stiffened Vivian's spine. She didn't have to see beyond the door to sense who stood there. "Oh no."

Jackson stepped back, his brows furrowed. "Are

you expecting your brother? He normally plows right on in."

Vivian's cheeks warmed. She had given Draven the wrong address the night before, not wanting him to learn where she lived. Especially now, with the ominous cloud over her head. She had no intention of keeping their date, but obviously her subterfuge had failed. He'd found her. Despite the feet of distance and the door between them, her body reacted to his nearness.

Vivian spun toward her bedroom. "I'm not here."

She shut herself in before Jackson could question her. With her back pressed to the door, eyes closed, heart beating faster than normal and her belly filled with butterflies, she listened to Jackson greet their guest.

To her utter dismay, she heard Fawn's sweet voice reciprocate his greeting.

"Jackson Emery, this is Draven Lourdes. He's an old friend of Kalen and Vivian's father," Fawn introduced.

A faint wisp of breeze fluttered her hair. When she opened her eyes, Kalen stood before her, his gaze pained but his expression filled with resolve. His powers intensified daily, and this newly acquired ability to move through walls was astonishing. He held out his arms. Vivian fell into her brother's embrace, soothed by his strength. There were so few moments when he could not comfort her, but right now, the thrum of his power and the warmth of his arms did wonders for her torn and tattered emotional reserves.

"I'm quite surprised, and impressed, by your tactics with him, dear sister," Kalen murmured into her hair. "He came by shortly after sunset inquiring about you after his apparent humiliating attempt to locate you at the wrong house."

"I don't want to involve him in this," Vivian said.

"Would you like me to tell him to get lost?"

Vivian chewed her lower lip. She knew she should. Let Draven go. Make him believe she had no interest in him. He deserved someone who wasn't plagued by a madman's poison.

Kalen's soft chuckle resonated within that beacon of light deep inside her soul. The one Draven created. The one that held more significance than her dismal future.

"That's what I thought." Kalen stepped back, bringing his hands to rest on her shoulders. "Vivi, your happiness is as important to me as mine is to you. We are not sacrificing ourselves. Not over this setback. Do you hear me? Do not give Hamstead the satisfaction. Now, you have a man waiting to take you out on a date. I think it'll do you some good."

"You've had a change of heart since last night." She nuzzled her cheek against the back of his hand. "I'm curious as to the reason why."

Kalen shrugged one shoulder. "Faunalyn has a way of making me see things her way." He raised his brows, the corners of his mouth curling in a small grin. "And he showed me respect enough to ask for help locating you, as well as permission to take you on a proper date."

Vivian lowered her head as she smiled. "Have you joined teams with him?"

"That remains to be seen, but it appears Faunalyn has."

*Of course she has.* Fawn believed the bond she shared with Kalen would manifest between Draven and Vivian.

But what were the chances?

"I should change," Vivian finally said, bringing her gaze up to meet her brother's. He tenderly tucked a lock of hair behind her ear before placing a light kiss on her forehead. "I don't think my flannel pants will do."

"I think they'll do fine. And an oversized sweatshirt," he teased. "Something really baggy and shapeless. I'll be in the kitchen with Jackson and Draven."

Vivian was about to ask about Fawn when a soft knock cut her off. Fawn stepped into the room the moment Kalen pulled open the door, then slipped past his fiancée.

Fawn's eyes glittered with lavender and gold, a rose blush on her cheeks. "So, Draven wants to take you to dinner. I told him Café Claude is the perfect place. Can I help you pick out an outfit?"

How could she deny Fawn the pleasure, especially when she saw how much it excited her close friend and sister-to-be?

Fifteen minutes of fussing later, Vivian was dressed in a black and gold halter-top dress that hugged her body and flared at the waist. It barely reached her knees, and definitely enhanced her cleavage. The heels Fawn had chosen for her made her normally shorter legs look miles long. The woman did something magical with her hair, creating a style with minimal pins and time and effort.

Still curious as to where the outfit had come from—Vivian did not remember seeing the dress in her closet a day ago—she tilted her head as Fawn stepped behind her and draped a thin gold chain with a gold-encased moonstone around her neck.

"I was saving it for a special day," Fawn said, smiling at Vivian's reflection in the mirror. Vivian lifted her hand and gingerly touched the stone, her eyes stinging. There wasn't the power she had felt in Kalen's circlet—the relic passed from their mother that signified their royal status among the Celestial fae—but there was certainly a thrum, a vibration of energy within the stone. "Today is as good as any. You look stunning, Vivi."

Staring at the image in the mirror, the swell of emotions that threatened her was indescribable.

"When did the dress come?" she asked, her voice thick.

"Ask your brother. We were in town earlier today and when I saw it at Into The Woods, he insisted on buying it for your date tonight."

"*Kalen* insisted?" She imaged he would regret his choice of attire once he saw her in the dress.

Fawn smiled. "I think Draven's grown on him."

He must have slipped it into her closet before she realized he had come into the room. She felt her own powers increasing, but not to the extent of Kalen's, which was fine. She was content just living.

Hopefully.

"Ready?" Fawn asked.

Vivian nodded. She turned to Fawn and wrapped her arms around the woman in a tight hug. Fawn laughed quietly, returning the hug.

"Vivian, everything will be fine. Promise me something." Fawn leaned back and caught her eyes. "Promise me you will not give Draven up."

Vivian stared at Fawn, her request touching her uncertain emotions. Her grin faltered.

"I had asked Kalen to promise me the same thing. With you."

Fawn's grin grew and she nodded. "I know. And he did. As should you. Don't give up. *Never* give up."

Vivian swallowed a lump in her throat. The corner of her eye twitched. "I won't."

Gods, she hoped she could keep that promise.

# Chapter 9

Draven had to catch his jaw before he gaped like an imbecile.

Actually, he simply rubbed his hand over his mouth to hide the gape that took over when Vivian paused in the archway leading to the kitchen. His skin prickled with a warning look from Kalen while his blood sizzled in his veins.

Vivian was nothing shy of a goddess in a sinful dress that showed off her subtle curves and fine cleavage. It was hard to miss, since her fingers played nervously with the pendant resting in the lush valley of her breasts. Her pale, almost luminescent skin took on a snowy rose blush that damn near sent him reeling. Her legs…those heels…her hair…

Draven dragged his hand down his mouth and chin, slipping behind the kitchen counter to hide his obvious reaction. He blinked, but the stunning image of the woman in the archway didn't vanish as he half expected.

Her diamond-like blue eyes lifted to his and he swore he felt a bolt of electricity shoot through his chest, trying to start his heart. Shame the thing was dead. He wondered how it would have reacted if it pumped.

Vivian's pulse certainly did a bit of a dance. That much he could hear and see.

As well as the obvious ogling of Jackson's gaze.

Despite assurances from both Jackson and Kalen that Jackson and Vivian were just friends, Draven wasn't born yesterday. She lived with the guy, and he obviously felt some non-platonic affection for her. He was a guy. Draven knew the signs, however stifled they may be.

"Good thing you brought a car." Fawn motioned to Vivian. "Since she's not in appropriate attire for riding."

Somehow, Draven believed Fawn and Kalen made certain of that. The final product was more than he could have ever imagined.

*Wonder if they realized she might be more dangerous to me like this than in jeans.*

He began to doubt his own confidence in the presence of this majestic woman. He knew without conceit he was someone to look at, but did he even stand a chance with her?

"You're gawking," Kalen whispered as he brushed behind him. He stepped up to his fiancée and took her in his arms.

Draven quickly cleared his throat. "Well, I think you've rendered me speechless, Miss Hawkins."

Her cheeks darkened. "I take it that's a feat hard to come by?"

Draven shrugged, trying to dispel a sudden bout of nerves. He approached Vivian and held out a hand. Vivian placed hers in his and he leaned over, pressing a kiss to her knuckles.

"Depends who you ask. I hope you're hungry?"

Vivian flashed her brother a shadowed glance before nodding. "Famished."

He spread his arm toward the door. "Shall we?"

"By all means."

Draven followed Vivian from the house, all of his previous questions and curiosities forgotten as he watched the woman glide down the stairs and the walkway. The moon cast her in a warm light, her hair appearing silvery white and her skin taking on a strange, almost ethereal glow. He stole a casual glance at his own hand, mentally noting the stark difference. The moon was nearly full, a large, fascinating orb with a thin sliver missing from one edge.

"Is everything okay?"

Draven jerked, unaware his steps had slowed as he took in the moonlight and the way it poured over Vivian. He was quick to remind himself they were not alone, the potent reminder of being watched piercing him through the back like a lance. His hat was off to Kalen as a contender for a Brother of the Year award.

"Of course, love."

Vivian's lips parted and her luminescent eyes widened slightly. Sweet gods, those eyes sucked him in like a mystical vortex. They were even brighter in the moonlight, those diamonds gleaming unnaturally. He brushed aside her surprise—quite honestly, the ease with which the endearment slipped from his lips startled him, as well—by closing the distance between them and guiding her to the sedan with a light hand on her lower back. Sparks of desire instantly jolted through him, and he had to bite back the urge to start the evening with a kiss that would surely have Kalen tearing him to into very small pieces.

"Here you go," Draven said softly, opening the door and holding her hand as she settled into the passenger seat. He waited until she was situated before closing the door and rounding the front bumper to the driver's side. He looked up at the house where Kalen and Fawn stood on the stoop. Fawn wore a bright smile while Kalen's toothy grin spoke volumes in silent warning. He chuckled as he dropped behind the wheel of the car. "Your brother would skin me if he could."

Vivian laughed. The sound was as airy and lulling as a soft breeze.

Heat stirred inside his otherwise cool veins.

He started the car and pulled away from the curb. Vivian waved to her brother and Fawn, then dropped her hands into her lap.

"I don't think you have anything to worry about," she confided. "This date wouldn't be taking place otherwise."

"I dare say he's more protective than I am. And that's admitting something."

"You and Kalen have many similarities. And yes, he's very protective. We've been through much together."

Was that sadness in her voice?

Draven clearly recalled Kalen telling him she had been hurt, along with their mention of a lab and a Dr. Hamstead. He'd learn about her past. He'd earn her trust. The drive to have her accept him and be his was unreasonable, but it overwhelmed him. He wanted Vivian.

No. It was stronger than that. Not an obsession, but a...a...

Need.

Somehow, she fed his soul the same way blood fed his body. Until he bumped into her at Howler's, he hadn't realized he was missing this other necessity to life. Now, he couldn't do without it.

"I should compliment you on your perseverance. You aren't one to give up easily, are you?" Vivian said, her voice lifting and casting away the heavy air that seemed to hover between them.

"Never was a quitter." He chuckled. "And if you're referring to my going to your brother to ask for help finding you, yeah. I was determined to bring you out on a proper date. You know, they say third time's a charm."

"I'm beginning to think anything that involves you is a charm."

He touched a hand to his chest in exaggerated pleasure. "Why, thank you."

She nudged him with her elbow and laughed.

Draven caught her hand, weaving their fingers together. The tingles and sparks that rode through his arm and settled in his gut made his vision fade momentarily. His mouth went dry. He eased off the accelerator until he could see the road again. An uncharacteristic ache started in his gums that followed the descent of his fangs.

A new hunger seized him. Not one to satiate the thirst, but one to satiate this new and unnamed need.

He cleared his throat, willing his fangs back.

"Why didn't you want to tell me where you lived?" Draven asked in a poor attempt to distract himself from his merciless hunger.

Vivian shrugged. "It's complicated."

"Because of Jackson?"

She tossed him a warm glance. "Jackson is a dear friend. His uncle helped Kalen and I through a very difficult time before he died. And Jackson has continued to help us. He's the least of your worries, romantically, if that's what you're referring to."

Sharp woman.

"I'm not worried, per se. I mean, I saw the way he looked at you. But who wouldn't have stopped breathing the moment you walked into the room?" He gave her a quick glance from head to toe. "You're a breathtaking sight. Both in looks and presence." He winked, pleased by the blush his words brought to her cheeks. "I think I might become addicted."

"Why, thank you, Mr. Lourdes, charmer extraordinaire."

He balked only an instant before letting out a roar of laughter. Vivian's eloquent laughter mixed with his, creating a symphony that sang to that hungry place in his soul. That same place that wanted to kiss her mad, and maybe a little more. A lot more.

*You're a danger to my self-control.*

Her hand squeezed his. "How am I a danger?"

Draven blinked. His foot eased off the accelerator and he looked at her. "Can you read minds?"

"You spoke aloud." Her delicate brow furrowed. "I wasn't supposed to hear that, huh?"

*Well, damn.*

"There go a few cards in my hand." He swore his own cheeks warmed. Yet, the sparkle in Vivian's eyes was more innocent and demure than that of a woman who knew the value of the information he unwittingly shared.

That innocence again.

So much conflict in this woman. So much he wanted to know and learn. So many questions stirred from their brief, and rather intense, encounters.

"I'm sure you'll do just fine with your loss. Somehow, I sense you have an overabundance of said cards at your disposal."

Draven glanced at her, sharing a smile at her playfulness. "I think I may just toss them all to the wind where you're concerned."

Vivian perched their elbows on the console between them. She gazed peacefully at their laced fingers.

"Good. I was never good at cards anyhow," she murmured. "Or games."

He tucked that small piece of information in his ever-growing mental file on this gorgeous woman. He leaned over and kissed the tips of a few of her fingers. "No games, Vivian. I promise."

And with that heartfelt vow, he closed the door on his single days in hopes of opening a new door into a life with Vivian Hawkins.

# Chapter 10

A dream.

Everything felt like a dream.

Café Claude was romance brought to life. The table Draven procured was intimate, tucked beneath a dimly lit chandelier. The tablecloth was smooth white, set with fine crystal and fancy dishware. A candle sat in the center, adding to the elegant ambiance and the intimate air.

However, nothing compared to the handsome man sitting across from her, swirling red wine in his glass.

Vivian had barely been able to maintain some semblance of calm when she saw Draven in Jackson's kitchen. He dressed up well. Maybe too well. He'd neatened his hair away from his face, but stubborn strands had retaken their rightful place over his blue eyes. His black pants fit him to perfection, making her suspect they were tailored to fit his long, lithe legs and rather enticing rear. His shirt was black, as well, a silk button-down open at the neck. The contrast to his pale skin was sharp and exotic, and turned quite a few female heads. He had worn his leather jacket, but quickly relinquished the supple material to drape over her shoulders for the short walk from the car to the restaurant.

The subtle spicy scent that lingered around him now clung to her dress.

The scent encompassing her taunted her, making her secretly wish she sat beside Draven. Perhaps lean up against him.

Instead, she sipped the wine he had chosen from the list, delighted by the flavor. Although it had little effect on her, thanks to her genetics, it did help take the edge off her nerves.

Or maybe seeing that Draven was nervous too helped.

A server placed their appetizer on the table. Vivian leaned a little closer to the dish, trying to figure out what she was looking at. Some pre-dinner research might have come in handy. The server dished out a portion to her first, then to Draven before taking his leave.

"What did you say this was again?" Vivian asked. She hadn't been paying attention when he ordered, too enraptured by his relaxed demeanor and the breathtaking curl of his lips. She picked up her fork and nudged one of the scallops.

"Coquilles St. Jacques," he said, his gaze intent on her. The corner of his mouth remained vaguely curled, apparently amused by her prodding.

"You're not allowed to speak French anymore." The way those words rolled from his mouth elicited a lick of hot lava up her spine. His chuckle magnified that burn.

"That may be difficult, considering we're dining in a French restaurant. *C'est ca, mademoiselle?*"

Vivian suppressed the shiver of pleasure caused by that low, husky rumble and the thick accent and cut into one of the scallops. "Aren't you funny?"

He shrugged one shoulder. "I'm putting a smile on your face, so I must be halfway to funny."

She stopped before popping the piece of delicious-smelling food into her mouth to look at him. His eyes sparkled as he cut a piece of his own appetizer, never once looking down at his plate. His confidence, despite his underlying nervousness, won her over more than once. He wasn't cocky, like some of the men she'd encountered on the nights Fawn had taken her out. His was a characteristic she appreciated.

Draven chuckled softly and reached across the small table. His fingers folded over hers, lifting her fork with the dripping mushroom to her lips. She allowed him to guide it into her mouth, catching the sharp flare of his nostrils when she slipped the scallop from the prongs. His pupils widened, casting the blues in a sensual shadow.

His grin turned carnal.

She chewed slowly as he pulled his arm back and settled back in his chair. He watched her with hyper-focused interest. She couldn't explain what came over her, but she indulged in his unspoken desire, taking her time and thoroughly enjoying the sweetness of the scallop. She was no culinary expert, but she doubted the bite would have tasted so good if not for the attention it garnered from the man across the table. He heightened her senses to peak far beyond what she'd experienced before.

"Are you punishing me for teasing you?" he asked, his voice gravelly to the point she could almost feel it scraping pleasantly down her back. She caught the hint of fangs beneath his upper lip when he spoke, not that she understood why she would be punishing him. They drew her attention as she swallowed her small bite. Her thoughts drifted into uncharted waters as she wondered how it would feel to have those teeth bite...

"No."

Gods, she sounded like a strangled animal.

She washed down food that had decided it was the perfect time to stop moving down her throat with a sip of wine.

After a delicate attempt to clear her throat, she rested the fork on the side of the plate and tented her hands. She rested her chin lightly on her fingertips. "Why would I punish you?"

His eyes narrowed. "Did you enjoy it?"

"The punishment or the food?"

Oh, how wicked his grin turned. And the things it woke inside of her.

"I'm finding myself unprepared for you this evening," he confessed, although from the tinge of husk in his voice, she doubted it was a confession at all. After a long, drawn-out silence where he watched her to the point his gaze seduced her mind and caressed her face, he took a hefty gulp of wine and straightened in his chair. A faint rose touched his cheeks. Was it a true blush? Or just the shadows from the dim lighting?

He lifted the bottle of wine and tipped it toward her near-empty glass. "Care for more?"

"Thank you." She wiped a single drop from the lip of the glass after he finished pouring. "Tell me about your sister. I heard the affection in your voice last night when you mentioned her."

"Sophia. Ahh, my lovely Sophia." Draven chuckled, the electric zing in the air fading enough to allow her to breathe easier. "She's had a rough life. Most of…our kind don't know what it's like to live in the sunlight, so we don't miss it. Can't miss what you don't know, right?"

"I'm sorry for you. Daylight is beautiful."

Draven gave a small nod. "So I've gathered from pictures and magazines and such, but the night is beautiful in an entirely different way. My sister developed an allergy or severe sensitivity to artificial light in addition to sunlight. Her life is dark, by all meanings of the word. Firelight, and minimal moon light, are the only means of illumination that don't bring her harm."

Vivian's fingers pressed to her lips. Draven spoke with so much emotion it connected with her own, igniting a sadness she had sensed in her brother.

Helplessness.

"Your father's family is pretty set in their ways. Like really, really old ways." He snorted softly. "Have you ever seen the old black-and-white Dracula movies?"

"I've seen one."

"Well, that's your family. Pristine coffins, frills and lace, dresses and frocks. They're pretty stuck in the nineteenth century. At least they have plumbing and electricity, though most of the time, it's not used."

Vivian scrunched her nose. "Why? The vampires I've met here are very modern."

"Trust me, I've tried to wrap my head around it for decades."

"Was my father like that? He didn't appear stuffy in the picture you showed us."

Draven cut off another piece of his appetizer, ate it, washed it down, and dabbed the linen napkin at the corner of his mouth. "Your father was trying to start a movement toward more modern living arrangements. That's why I liked him so much. He had connections with specialists and tried to find a cure for Sophia before he was taken." He shook his head, his gaze lowering with a flash of coolness. "I still can't understand *how* he was taken."

"Drugs can do much damage, even to the strongest of us." She regretted her words the moment his attention shot up to her. She shrugged and looked away. "I assume."

Oh, she'd spoken too much. His piqued expression told her so.

"Did the people who took Sal take you and your brother? Is that the lab you mentioned last night?"

Memories, fierce and horrific, stabbed at her mind. She wasn't going to allow this night, her first real date with a man that calmed and coaxed her like a longtime friend, go the way of the gutter.

"Were the specialists able to find a cure for your sister? Or does she still suffer her ailments?"

Draven gauged her expression for a long moment. Vivian used the silence to indulge in another bite of the mouthwatering mushroom and scallop dish.

"Jackson is a microbiologist, you know. He might be able to lend a hand," she continued, ignoring the curiosity probing her from across the table. "I'm sure I can speak with him to see if he'd be able to lend insight."

"That's very kind of you, but I wouldn't want to impose on your friend."

"He's practically family."

"I'll keep that in mind, then. Thank you."

She smiled. "I hope I have the opportunity to meet your sister. Your fondness for her assures me she's a special woman."

Admiration lit his eyes, dimming his curiosity. "She's beautiful. There are some aspects of you that remind me of her. Very soft-spoken and polite. Playful yet serious. Thoughtful. Immensely thoughtful. There are times I wonder if I'm really the older sibling because the things that come out of her mouth make me question my own intelligence." He smirked. Vivian raised a brow in sync with the corner of her mouth. "And I'd like to think I rank up there pretty high when it comes to brains."

"French brains?"

"Oh, now you've gone and ruined my confidence."

They shared a stifled bout of laughter, and further taunts and light conversation about the town and intelligence. Vivian sighed inside with each slip of French Draven skillfully interjected into the conversation, as well as Spanish and old Gaelic. The entrees came and neither one touched the rich-smelling dishes, choosing conversation and wine over moments of silence to eat.

"I wouldn't have guessed you to be Irish."

Draven's brows rose. "Oh? Why not?"

"I don't know." Heat rose to her cheeks. "I'm not really versed in different cultures and nationalities."

"Well, I still think you're descended from the ancient gods."

She wagged a finger. "Now, now. You may be closer to your mark than you think."

"Well." Draven pushed his dish aside and perched his elbows on the table. "I consider myself to be humbly in the presence of a goddess, whether you are or you're not. My impression of you won't change. And, just for the record, my mother is Irish. My father is French. That's where Lourdes comes from."

She reached across the table and traced the angular bone of his jaw. "That's where this elegant structure comes from."

"You've got a dangerous touch, Vivian." He tapped the tip of a finger against the bowl of his wine glass. "And I've had a dangerous amount of wine."

She tsked. "Wine has no effect on you and you know it."

"Perhaps not, but I'm going to leave the warning there."

In the past, she would have recoiled at the word. Nothing good ever came of a warning unheeded.

But Draven's warning drew on her curiosity and that simmering heat that stoked low in her belly from the instant she saw him in the kitchen at Jackson's house.

"Tell me about your mother."

She frowned and her inner heat dissipated. She settled back in her chair, her hands cupping the bottom of her wine glass.

"I don't remember much about her except she was beautiful."

"You inherited her fine traits."

"I suppose."

"Do you remember where she's from?"

Neither she nor her brother knew much about their Celestial background because there wasn't much in any book to learn from. Her mother's breed was as elusive as a ghost might be to a human. Some had the opportunity to see and meet the Celestial fae, while others believed them to be nothing more than tall tales. One thing that became apparent during their hunt for Dr. Hamstead before he was apprehended: The circlet, their mother's crown, held the source of power for them. If that fell into the wrong hands, the consequences could be devastating.

"Her past was a bit...complex, or so I've been told," Vivian finally answered, diverting her gaze from Draven's. It wasn't a lie, but she didn't want him pressing for more information. Not here, in the middle of a restaurant.

"Well, if she looked anything like you, I can see why Sal fell for her," Draven said softly.

"I wish I had known him." When Draven slid his plate in front of him again, she looked up. "What was he like?"

Draven lifted his fork and knife and used the tines of his fork to motion toward her plate. "This looks amazing, and it's getting cold. I'll tell you about Sal while you eat."

# Chapter 11

Draven busied himself recapturing memories of Sal to share with Vivian while she ate with the daintiness of a princess. He kept the conversation light-hearted, averting his gaze from her mouth or the ample cleavage that deepened when she moved certain ways. There was an undeniable pull, a connection between them that they both acknowledged, but tried to keep at bay. He, out of respect for Vivian. Her, for whatever secrets she continued to withhold.

He decided he loved the sound of her laughter, so light and airy and musical. He loved the way her eyes twinkled when she smiled. Loved the strokes of rose that crossed her delicate cheeks. He thoroughly enjoyed her banter and was completely taken by the serenity of her essence.

He was a foolhardy man who had fallen for a woman.

Not just any woman, but Vivian Hawkins. A glorified beauty with a spirit of gold, a mind as complex as her mother's apparent breeding, and an innocence he wanted to protect.

The rest of their date went smoothly, albeit too fast, even if they closed out Café Claude. Draven made sure to leave a hefty tip in thanks for the staff's patience. He considered extending the evening to one of the clubs Clark had told him about, but was wary of the temptation that would come with any intimate atmosphere.

Sure, he'd love to indulge, but refused to disrespect Vivian to feed his own desires. It was bad enough the temptation rocked him more times that he cared to count over dinner, and that was in a public domain that was romantic, but not necessarily seductive.

He could only imagine what the thump of music, fog, dim lights, and sofas might do.

He directed the loaner car from Clark into the driveway of Jackson's house and cut the engine. He flashed Vivian a smile before climbing out of the car to help her from her seat. He didn't relinquish her hand as they walked to the front door.

"I had a wonderful time tonight, Draven," Vivian said, resting her head against his arm for a moment. "Thank you."

"If you're up for it, I'd love to see you again. Tomorrow night."

He led her up to the stoop and turned to face her. As at many times throughout the evening, she captivated him, striking away the world, leaving Vivian and him beneath the glow of the moonlight.

Yeah, the club wouldn't have been a good idea at all. He couldn't help himself when he cupped her face between his palms and brushed his thumb over her lower lip. The slow, sensual motion left those lips parted on a breath and her hands resting over his.

"I'd like that."

The corner of his mouth twitched. "Pants. Jeans. Something to cover your legs." He dipped his head, nuzzling his nose against hers in a light caress. "I'll take you on the bike, if you'd like."

"Do I look like I seek thrills?" she teased, leaning her small frame closer. "I'll cover my legs."

Draven tilted his head and covered her mouth with his. Fire exploded along his nerves, scalding his veins and searing his mind. Oh, sweet heavens, the way she met each sweep of his tongue, a powerful give and take in a dance that quickly spiraled out of control. She tasted like wine and light and inspired a craving he never wanted to satiate.

He didn't recall dropping his hand to her lower back and bringing her flush against him. Her body, so warm and delicate, felt damn right in his arms. His palm molded perfectly along her face.

Their mouths melded together as if meant for one another.

"Ahem."

Vivian jerked, tearing her mouth away. Draven secured her to him, refusing to allow the impromptu interruption from Jackson, who appeared rumpled and rather annoyed in the open doorway, to end their evening on a sour note. He had to bite back a satisfied grin when she relaxed into his chest and rested her head beneath his chin.

Jackson's brows rose over his glasses. He glowered at Draven for a long moment before turning a far kinder expression on Vivian.

It made Draven growl inside.

"I was waiting for you two to come back. I need to discuss some…things with you, Vivi." That softness he turned on Vivian froze over as he lifted his gaze back to Draven. "I'm sorry to cut this night short." He didn't sound sorry in the least.

Vivian patted Draven's hand before she stepped out of his arms. She smiled at him. "Tomorrow. I'll be waiting."

Draven mustered a smile for Vivian's sake, ignoring the coolness in Jackson's expression. "Nine?"

"Nine is perfect. Thank you for a wonderful evening. I'll see you tomorrow."

Draven waited on the walkway at the foot of the stoop as Vivian disappeared inside the house. Jackson rolled his eyes and firmly closed the door.

"You're just jealous," Draven groused at the door, kicking a pebble into the stair with the toe of his shoe.

The night's abrupt ending succeeded in putting Draven in a foul mood. That mood plummeted into the pits of disgust when he returned to Clark's house, stepped into the kitchen, and saw three black-clad, cloak-wearing, pasty-skinned men sitting like stiff corpses at Clark's counter.

*Well, Death has decided to pick a ripe night for a visit.*

The vampires turned like one being divvied up into three to watch as he made his entrance. Clark turned his eyes to the ceiling with an arch of his brows as he pushed off his elbows at the counter and straightened onto his feet. Draven tossed Clark's car keys and his friend caught them flawlessly.

Not a single vampire flinched.

Garrett, his obsidian eyes sharp, nodded in greeting. "Draven. I do hope we aren't intruding. We've arrived earlier than expected."

"I see that. I wasn't expecting you for another night or so." Draven went to the fridge and pulled out beers for Clark and himself. "Drink?"

Elders Brodan and Sylvester lifted their hands in unison to decline the offer. Their skeletal features and deep-set black eyes could rival those of a corpse. *It's a good thing they can't walk in the sunlight. These men would scare the life from the living.*

Draven popped the cap off his beer and took a swig. If only beer had even a fraction of the effect on him as it did on humans, he'd appreciate the relaxing buzz.

"Have you explored the town?" Draven asked. Clark snickered behind the lip of his bottle as he tipped the beer up for a drink. Garrett cast Clark a frozen glance before turning that dead gaze to Draven. Gods, what he'd do to return to Vivian, if only to steal a glimpse of the life and emotion in her eyes. To feel her *warmth.* "I assume not."

"We do not have reason to explore. We are here for

one purpose, that of which I hope you have discovered some evidence for us."

"Well, I've actually been enjoying the bars and the clubs. I was going to get to work tomorrow."

Brodan's lips pulled tight. "There is no time to waste should there be a chance Salvatore is alive."

Draven scowled. Despite these guys taking him and his family under their roof, he never cared for them. It was as if they walked a tightrope through their utterly boring lives. They moved from point A to point B without so much as enjoying the scenery along the way.

Such a waste of immortality.

"Sal's dead. He fathered two children who have inherited his accounts. That is why the accounts haven't been touched until recently. They only came into the inheritance, from what I've learned."

Garrett shared a silent glance with his two sidekicks. Draven hopped up onto the edge of the counter and leaned back against the cabinets. Clark groaned.

"You've forgotten your manners," he mumbled.

Draven flashed him an exaggerated smile and toasted the air with his beer. "To your reckless and inconsiderate friend."

Clark laughed, taking up a spot on the counter opposite the sink.

Garrett cleared his throat to recapture Draven's attention. What the old bones didn't realize was his attention barely hung on Garrett's presence and was entirely focused on Vivian.

He couldn't wait until tomorrow evening.

"Have you...met these children of his? Have you confirmed this to be true?"

"Clark has some sources in town capable of confirming this," Draven said. He caught himself before he added the siblings weren't purebred vampires. Instead, he toed the subject with a casual, "Maybe they walk in the sunlight and sleep at night. Nowadays, with *modern* technology, anything's possible."

Sylvester scowled, his white teeth and sharp fangs creating a monster out of the man. "Salvatore would never allow his children to tamper in beliefs beyond our coven."

Draven gave himself an exaggerated once-over before meeting Sylvester's disgusted gaze. "I'm certainly not entirely of your coven's beliefs, but I landed in your house."

Garrett straightened up more, if that was even possible. "Draven, do not disrespect the Elders."

He shrugged. "I speak nothing but the truth and offer one of the numerous possibilities that might involve Sal's offspring. We don't know what happened to him once he left Levoire Mansion. We don't know whom he met, where he went, and who is responsible for his death. The name of the woman with whom he produced these children." He leaned forward, elbows on his knees with his beer resting lightly between his hands. "What if his children aren't pure vampires? What if the mother was something other than one of us? I mean no disrespect by stating the obvious,

Garrett, but remaining stuck in a time from two centuries ago is an enemy you don't want to dance with."

"Draven—"

He held up a stalling hand. "One more thing, if I may. What I've seen of this town so far is unlike anything I've experienced elsewhere. There are supernaturals of all kinds, many of whom are not dating, engaged, or married to members of their own races or breeds. Just keep that in mind."

He needed to definitively know Garrett's stance on crossbreeds. What dangers might be presented to Vivian and her brother when the old bones discovered the truth.

Garrett remained stone still. Had Draven not known him to be a living…thing, he'd think the guy was a Halloween decoration. It would certainly fit with the town's theme, as well as the time of year.

"It is not something we will consider. Salvatore's heirs are purebred of his bloodline. He would never sacrifice his place, or the future of his coven, by diluting the Levoire blood with that of a lesser breed."

Garrett's declaration raked away any good humor that remained inside Draven. Slowly, he placed his beer on the counter and wrapped his hands around the granite edge. His nails dug into the solid material. The air crackled with tension.

"It's a possibility, Garrett, a very real one. If, and I speak hypothetically"—*you blasted screwball*—"I come to learn his children are not purebred vampires, what will you do? They are all that is left of Sal, and the rightful heirs to the coven, regardless of their breeding."

"They will be terminated and a new heir will be chosen at our discretion," Brodan said instantly.

Draven gave a nonchalant shrug as a slew of cusses echoed through his head. He worried that Vivian and Kalen wouldn't be welcomed with open arms, but he didn't expect these ancient cadavers to call down a damn death sentence without any consideration.

"We cannot have any threat to our beliefs," Sylvester said, his voice as cold as his skin. "We have thrived by our laws and that cannot be jeopardized."

Draven may have tolerated these guys and their old ways before. Now? In addition to mentally devising a plan to keep Vivian and Kalen under Garrett's radar, he wanted to get Sophia out of Levoire Mansion. He knew in his heart his parents would never leave, but if he could save his sister from the dismal future these three planned, he would.

"We shall return tomorrow evening," Garrett said, his voice adding to the tension in the room. The three stood in unison, one being divided into three. All three pairs of cold, dead eyes stared at him. "Our gratitude for your service to us and your continued help in this matter."

Draven seethed as the Elders filed out of the kitchen like ghosts floating in black cloaks.

When Garrett reached the front door, Draven dropped to his feet. "I *do* have another question for you."

Garrett paused, but didn't turn.

Draven took one step toward him. "When you suspected there might have been heirs, did you consider bringing them back to the mansion might not fit with your plans for the coven's future?"

The dark idea swelled within him, making his stomach tilt. In that moment of clarity, he realized how blind he had been coming into this mission.

"We never considered bringing any child of Salvatore's back to the mansion. They were not raised under our laws." Garrett turned his head just enough to catch Draven's gaze from the corner of his eye. "This is about justice and eliminating any threat to the future head of the coven. We must clean up the mistakes of the past to ensure the future of the Levoire family. Good evening."

Shards of razor-like ice raked through his veins as he stared at the empty space where Garrett had stood. The front door closed quietly. He'd been used as a proverbial hunting hound for the judge, jury, and executioner.

*You damn son of a—*

"Easy." Clark flicked his hand.

Draven looked down at his fist, his arm trembling. Small drops of blood fell to the floor by his shoe. He relaxed his fingers, his nails unlatching from his palm, and gave his skin time to heal.

"Well, guess there won't be any familial introductions occurring anytime soon." Clark's sarcasm was weighted with the same fury that beat within Draven. "How did your date go?"

Draven hissed, baring his fangs. "I'm going to maul that damn skeletal excuse for a placeholder in this world. Give him a damn UV bath."

Clark scowled. "I'll help you pull back the curtains."

"I need a drink." He slammed his fist on the counter and growled as cracks appeared in it. Any hope of retaining some calm from his time with Vivian vanished on the wings of his new rage and worry. "A *real* drink."

Thank the gods for his friend. Clark was the closest person to family besides Draven's blood family.

"I know a place in town that's open late and serves up some spiked red wine."

Draven was at the door before Clark finished talking. "Let's go. I'll clean up the blood when we get back."

# Chapter 12

Saturday morning blueberry pancakes at Mummy's Diner. A small tradition that brought a smile to Vivian's mouth and excitement to the beginning of another day.

Except for today.

Tucked in a booth with Jackson beside her and Fawn and Kalen opposite them, she couldn't muster much excitement. Apparently, neither could anyone else. Anxiety thrummed between them, dense and suffocating. Not even the sweet smell of pancakes could tease her mouth to water or will away the unease stirring her belly.

Jackson glanced at his watch. Again. He lifted his coffee mug for a sip, but put it down before actually drinking.

Vivian lowered her fork to the table, giving up on breakfast. She finally looked at her brother, whose haunting gaze had watched her hawkishly for the last ten minutes. She'd been avoiding his worried look.

"Jackson, one minute. Sixty seconds. Give your arm a rest before I take that watch off your wrist," Fawn said, pushing her barely-touched pancakes to the side with a sigh. Jackson grumbled something under his breath as he dropped his hand on the table.

"Vivi," Kalen murmured, his voice soft and comforting, a promise of support not in words but in the tone and the emotion behind his nickname for her. She forced a small smile, acknowledging what he was trying to do. He'd done it so many times before when they were prisoners at the lab. A secret embrace through one single word and all the love he held for her behind that word when he spoke.

"A setback is not the end. Mustn't forget that," Fawn finally said, addressing everyone's dour mood directly. "This will get figured out and fixed. For good."

"It's hard to fix something that hides," Jackson groused, tugging a hand through his hair. The mussed strands stood up in every direction until he smoothed them down, not that it helped much. He looked at Vivian. "I think it would be a good idea not to bring Douglas arou—"

"Draven," Vivian corrected.

Jackson waved a hand. "Draven. Until we have this controlled. You know, just in case there are any moments where you regress."

"Jealously doesn't play well on you, Jackson," Kalen said, his voice taut. Jackson's cheeks reddened, but he met Kalen's gaze without flinching.

KIRA NYTE

"I'm being serious. One of the variables from my blood samples regressed twice as fast as the day before. Like math. Today is one-plus-one, tomorrow is two-plus-two, the following day four-plus-four. You see? At this rate, the loss of control could happen sooner than later, and almost without warning." Jackson blew out a breath. "I'm *not* jealous, Kalen."

"You're as *not* jealous as I am *not* smitten."

Fawn snorted a laugh. Vivian's eyes widened.

"Oh, don't go there." Jackson twisted to look at Vivian, his eyes pleading and his face flushed. "I'm not jealous. Really. Your brother needs some manners."

Vivian patted the back of Jackson's hand. "I know you're not." She knew very well he was. "He's just concerned. We're all concerned."

"That's one hell of a strange way of showing concern when his jab was directed at me." He pushed his glasses up on the bridge of his nose. "Regardless, I think I'm going to head over to Hugh's. Sitting here is doing me no good. I'll see you there."

Vivian sighed inwardly when Jackson dropped a twenty onto the table, slid out of the booth, and disappeared through the crowded lobby area.

"You won't let it go, brother." She turned her dismayed gaze to Kalen. At least he had the sense to appear apologetic. "It was nothing but a small kiss. Nothing but me being curious. He was not at fault."

"I'm aware, Vivi. That doesn't change the fact that part of him lusts for you," Kalen said quietly. A knowing gleam lit his irises when he shared a loving look with Fawn. "Sometimes, what we think is simple is far more than that." He took Fawn's hand in his and kissed her fingertips. "Perhaps we can bring him out one night. To that club you've told me about. Insomnia, correct?"

"It might do him some good," Fawn agreed. This time, she glanced at her watch. "Hugh said we should come by around eleven. It's quarter of." She smiled at Vivian. "What do you say?"

"I'm ready to see what he's developing."

Kalen paid the server, tucking Jackson's money into Vivian's hand. "Give it back to him." As they climbed out of the booth, her brother slung an arm around her shoulders. "How did everything go last night with Draven?"

Vivian smiled, the first genuine expression she'd mustered since waking up this morning. "Nice. We had an enjoyable time at Café Claude. And just so you know, Jackson made sure Draven didn't do anything he shouldn't have when we got home."

Kalen snickered. "Good."

"You know that's not going to be the case for long, especially if they're like us," Fawn warned. Kalen released Vivian's shoulders to hold open the door to the diner with a scowl. Fawn gathered one of Vivian's hands and winked. "When are you seeing him again?"

"Tonight."

"Sweatpants and a sweatshirt," Kalen muttered.

Fawn waved him away. "Where are you going?"

Vivian laughed. Oh, what the very thought of Draven did to her. How it erased the dismal situation she faced. "He wants to take me for a ride on his motorcycle."

Fawn's eyes widened. "Oh, then I'll bring you shopping after we leave Hugh's." She nudged Kalen's arm. "Aren't you excited for your sister?"

Kalen's expression remained sharp and cool, but his eyes softened. He grunted noncommittally.

Vivian's smile grew. "Now, brother. Be kind. He was a complete gentleman last night. I'm sure he'll be even more so tonight."

"Yeah. Sure. I know what would be going through my mind if Faunalyn were sitting behind me on a bike."

"You're preaching innocence when you are far from a saint," Fawn teased Kalen. His eyes flashed, then took on a look Vivian had become very well acquainted with over dinner with Draven, and what that look did to her body. "All the more reason for extra layers, right, love?"

"A suit of armor would be a start."

Vivian paused by the door to the backseat of Fawn's car. "I fear for any daughters you and Fawn might have in the future. Especially if this is how protective you are of me, who is only your sister."

He kissed the top of her head. "You are my sweet Vivi. I would do anything to make sure you're safe. And happy."

Vivian didn't doubt him in the least. For as long as

she could remember, Kalen made her safety and happiness his responsibility.

"Let's see what new strategies Hugh has come up with to battle this latest version of Dr. Mad Scientist's mutation."

Delaney Ellingham placed a tray of fresh brownies on one of the tables in Hugh's lab and wiped her hands on the apron around her waist. "They're still warm."

Jackson leaned closer to the tray. He caught his glasses as they slid down his nose with the tip of his finger. "They're orange."

"They're white chocolate chip pumpkin brownies with caramel drizzle." Delaney's smile widened. "They've been a huge hit at the shop. Can't go wrong with pumpkin this time of year."

Vivian wished her stomach would stop churning. She'd love to dig into one of those delicious-looking brownies. Alas, her appetite fled her, as well as her short-lived good mood, the moment they pulled up the driveway to Hugh's enormous house. The last time she stood in this room, she was on the brink of falling victim to the monster inside her. Minutes had become crucial. Dr. Hamstead had been on the run.

Hugh descended the stairs to the basement lab with quick, graceful steps. His eyes darted between each person in the room, landing on Vivian last. A mixture of sympathy and determination set in his expression.

"My apologies for my delay. Something came up regarding the Black and Orange Ball." He crossed the room, pausing to shake Kalen's hand and offer Fawn a small hug. "Are you planning on attending?"

Fawn nodded. "I purchased tickets the day they went on sale. We're looking forward to it."

Hugh grinned. "Wonderful. Now, would anyone care for coffee, tea, or another beverage before we get started?"

Vivian wasn't the only one who suffered a tumultuous gut. Her brother passed up the chance for blood-laced wine and Jackson forewent the opportunity to sip on fine Scotch.

"I think we're good," Jackson said, choosing one of the brownie squares. He took a nibble and moaned. "Wow, Delaney. You've outdone yourself with these."

Delaney beamed. Hugh lifted his eyes to the ceiling. Vivian had a feeling he had been her taste tester to get the recipe right. She'd have to take one home to enjoy later.

"Thanks. Took me three days to get that recipe right."

"Three *and a half* days, actually," Hugh corrected.

"Well, on that note, I'll leave you be. I have to check on the little one."

The adoration in Hugh's expression as he watched his wife leave the lab made Vivian's heart swell. Oh, she hoped one day she would get a chance to share that kind of love with someone. Who was she kidding? With Draven.

Hugh turned to Jackson. "I've reviewed your results and notes over the last day, as well as your suggestions and in which direction they point. I agree that we need to somehow introduce a component to my last serum that would penetrate the viral wall and restructure the DNA from within." He stroked his chin for a thoughtful moment. "Seems that attacking it from the outside isn't doing much besides causing it to mutate."

"But I've been well for a few months now," Vivian said. She wasn't as knowledgeable as Jackson when it came to the science of this situation, but Hugh's words plucked a fearsome chord in her mind. "It came back?"

Hugh sighed. "Unfortunately, I believe all we succeeded in doing was forcing the virus into hiding until it changed its components to deflect my previous antidote." A frown tugged at the corners of his mouth. He asked Jackson, "Have you discussed anything with Vivian and Kalen?"

Jackson shook his head. "No. Not yet. I wanted to wait until we were all together. To keep things in order and avoid confusion."

"Very well." Hugh went to the sideboard and motioned to a tray of tea cups and a steaming pot. "Are you sure I can't offer anyone a drink?"

"Thank you, no," Vivian declined. Kalen and Fawn shook their heads. "Do you think we can cure this, Hugh?"

"I don't give up easily. Certainly not when one's life is at risk." Hugh returned and motioned to the seats set away from his worktable and cabinets of bottles and equipment. They all took chairs. "Do I believe there's a cure? Yes. It's all a matter of finding it. Unfortunately, it may take a few times before we get it right. If you might be open to the suggestion, allow me to discuss this with Alice Bishop and see if there is any amulet or talisman she might be able to forge to offset the effects of the virus until we've developed that cure. Nothing except a cure will be a permanent solution, but it'll help."

"I don't want the symptoms masked. I don't want to miss something and find out it's too late to do anything about it," Vivian said. She hated that she would suffer the effects of the virus more acutely, but everyone would have a better idea of the severity if she didn't hide what it was doing behind spells and witchcraft.

Hugh's mouth twitched at the corners. His eyes glinted with respect. "You are a strong woman, Vivian. That is to be admired."

She doubted she was strong in the sense he meant, but she smiled. His words gave her some hope.

"What will be required?" Kalen asked, shattering the momentary sentiment.

*Back to business.*

A stark reminder that time, even for an immortal, wasn't always an ally.

"I would like to take blood samples, as well as a small tissue sample to use in creating a potential cure. That way, we, Jackson and I, can follow either the progress or the failure of the chemical combinations we create."

Vivian suppressed a shiver. She shot Kalen a split-second glance and saw his jaw tighten and his eyes go dark.

The idea of Hugh retrieving a tissue sample brought back a storm of old memories from the lab. Memories Vivian didn't want to relive. Strapped to metal examination tables while doctors and scientists cut and scraped and poked. The pain, the agony, the humiliation and helplessness. Anesthetics had burned off too quickly to help. The doctors finally decided not to bother, leaving her to experience every slice of the scalpel. Every pierce of an instrument.

The shiver broke through her restraints.

*The pain.*

The secrets not even her brother knew.

She swallowed bile that rose in the back of her throat. Maybe a little wine wouldn't be such a bad idea. It would help with the blood thirst that hit her in waves as the beast grew stronger. Her thirst had never been as strong as Kalen's, but she was still part vampire, and that part of her required sustenance.

Hugh must have sensed her apprehension or caught a glimpse of her fear. He leaned forward in his chair, elbows on knees. "I have developed a type of block that will numb the area for a short time so I can obtain the sample. You shouldn't feel any pain. If for some reason it doesn't hold, then I won't obtain the sample. Having a sample of tissue to see how this virus plays inside your body will help us determine what we need to factor into the antidote."

"Okay. That's fine," Vivian agreed before she had time to dissuade herself. A sensation of chill caressed her arm. Her brother was severely unhappy with her decision, but he remained silent as she spoke on her own behalf. "Do you want to take the sample now?"

Hugh pressed his lips together. "If you'd be willing. Jackson and I agree that we shouldn't delay this any longer than necessary."

She nodded once, her gaze drifting toward her brother, then Fawn. "You'll still come shopping with me after this, right?"

Fawn smiled. "Of course, Vivi."

Well, at least she had something positive to anticipate to get her through these next few minutes.

# Chapter 13

Fawn certainly had ideas about proper bike attire. And they conflicted horribly with Jackson's.

Jackson stood in the doorway of his makeshift lab, his jaw grinding as he looked her over. His face turned a light shade of red. "Really? Has Kalen seen this outfit?"

"Kalen went to Magical Mayhem after leaving Hugh's house to pay invoices and see how Wendy and the new girl, Georgia, were doing. Fawn and I shopped alone." She frowned, holding her arms out at her sides. She glanced down at her ensemble—soft leather pants, low-heeled ankle boots, a deep red cashmere sweater with a low V cut, and a thigh-length leather jacket. "Is it that horrible?"

The throaty rumble of an engine made her heart kick up in pace. It drew closer quickly.

"Oh, I think he's here."

"Back to your clothes." Jackson whisked down the

hallway and took her by the shoulders. He spun her around and herded her back to her room.

The doorbell rang.

He pointed to the bedroom. "It's horrendous. He'll hate it. Who would ever consider leather for a ride on a motorcycle? And that sweater? I thought Fawn had better fashion sense."

"I'm sure she'd consult you for flannel."

"Yeah, thanks, Vivi." Jackson let out an exaggerated groan and rolled his eyes. "I'll keep him occupied while you change. That damn sweater is way too…red."

"But—"

Jackson gave her a gentle shove into the room. She spun around as he grabbed the doorknob and pulled the door shut, but not without pointing a finger toward her closet. "Change!"

Vivian stuck her tongue out at the closed door. She turned to the mirror over her dresser and looked at her choice of attire. She'd seen plenty of people wear leather on bikes. She assumed it was appropriate attire. Okay, so maybe the sweater *was* a little too red, but it was cute and warm. And soft. So, so soft.

What did the color of her sweater have to do with anything about riding a bike?

She fixed a few strands of hair that had come loose from the braids into the half ponytail around the tips of her ears. They still managed to escape and caress her cheeks, the edges blending into the surreal glow that suffused her bare skin tonight. Essence of the full moon, despite the dense cloud cover. Her eyes glowed bright, light blue with glittering silver.

"Momma, I trust in your wisdom," she whispered to the image staring back at her. Eyes that triggered memories of staring up from her mother's arms into a warm gaze. It made her heart ache, the memories, the loss. Even after all this time. Her mere age of two didn't obscure her memories as it would that of most humans. What she did remember was vivid and sharp, and made her wish she could have even five minutes with her mother.

Not only was tonight her second date with Draven, it was the night she hoped to learn if the connection that shimmered between them was rooted in something deeper. Something promising and eternal.

After a lengthy stretch of time to make Jackson believe she was changing, she emerged from her room and moved silently through the hallway until she reached the living room.

Draven and Jackson sat in chairs opposite each other. Both wore disgruntled expressions. The energy in the air was thick and heavy. Sparks flashed in Jackson's eyes and faint strands of light flitted across his fingertips, the only sign of his witchy breeding. To her astonishment, neither man moved, except for Jackson's chest with each breath. They watched each other like enemies preparing for battle…or chess.

Vivian knocked on the wall just inside the archway to the living room.

Draven's attention snapped to her and his eyes widened. "Vivian. Well…wow."

Jackson scowled. He slumped back in his chair and dropped his head on the back to stare up at the ceiling.

Draven appeared in front of her in a blink, taking her hands to kiss her knuckles.

"I was worried this wouldn't be appropriate motorcycle attire, but Fawn said it was perfect. Should I change?" Vivian asked.

"It certainly *is* perfect, love." He popped his knee up with the toe of his boot. "I usually wear leather on the bike."

It was sinful the way his leather pants showed off his narrowed waist and lithe thighs. They were boot-cut, if she recalled the term correctly, and fell straight from his knee to the top of his boots. As he lowered their hands, he stole a small tug at the bottom of her sweater, his nostrils flaring.

"This is quite nice on you."

Jackson shoved to his feet and rounded Draven's back. He caught Vivian's eyes as he stopped long enough to plant a chaste kiss to her cheek. "Be careful." He tossed Draven a cold glance. "Home in one piece, you hear?"

"Aye, aye, Captain," Draven teased.

Vivian released Draven's hand and squeezed Jackson's shoulder. "I'll be fine. If anything happens, I'll call you."

Jackson nodded and disappeared around the corner.

His demeanor sank into a desolate place, one that made her a little sad.

"You okay, love?"

Draven's worried tone snapped her out of her thoughts. She smiled up at him and nodded. "Of course. So, should I be worried about being on the back of a motorcycle with you?"

Draven's concern lifted, exposing a mischievous man in its stead. "That, my darling, depends on who you ask. Why don't you tell me when the night is over, hmm?"

A thrill curled through her belly. "Then let's get the night started."

Draven led her from the house and down the front walkway to the street. A big black-and-chrome beast of a machine waited beside the curb, a single black helmet on the passenger seat. He picked it up and pulled the straps aside before positioning it over Vivian's head. She hadn't realized she was holding her breath for the moment when their eyes met under the moonlight until a disappointed sigh escaped her lips. The moon remained hidden behind the clouds. There was no sign of anything but Draven's captivating blue in his irises.

A faint crease marred his brow. "Wait. I forgot something."

"What—"

His lips covered hers in a soft, tender kiss, but her body's reaction was anything but soft and tender. He might as well have ignited a torch inside her, for what that kiss did.

"You devastate me," he murmured against her lips.

"In a very good way."

*I think you do the same to me.*

He eased the helmet onto her head, taking care to move her hair from the straps before he secured the bulky piece of plastic in place. He took her hand and tossed his leg over the seat, settling in the saddle like a man born to ride. It was downright sexy to watch him situate himself while holding her hand.

"Hop on, love. Put your feet on the pegs once you're seated."

He pointed to a piece of metal protruding from the side of the bike, above the shining exhaust. Allowing him to guide her with her hand in his, she kicked her leg over the rear of the seat. She grabbed his shoulder with her free hand as she sat, getting a feel for the bike beneath her. A pulse of nervousness shot through her as she set her boots on the pegs. There was nothing to protect her except for her clothing, the helmet, and the man in front of her.

He brought their entwined hands under his arm and pressed her palm flat to his lower chest.

She swallowed hard, closing her eyes as her hand molded to the hard muscle beneath his shirt. The tips of her fingers spread slightly, following the dip at the center of his chest.

A playful tap against her hand resting on his shoulder drew her to open her eyes.

*Oh, sweet heavens.*

He was watching her in the mirror, a knowing grin playing across his lips.

"Wrap your arms around me and hold on. The faster we go, it'll be more comfortable to dip your head. Lean against me, into me. When we take turns, lean into them with me. Don't resist. It's how you steer a bike."

"It won't tip over?" she asked, slipping her other arm around his chest and locking her hands around her wrists. So far, she enjoyed the ride.

He chuckled. "I have a tad bit of know-how when it comes to handling this beast."

As if to prove his point, he kick-started the bike into a roar, and said beast rumbled beneath her legs.

"Keep away from the exhaust pipes. They'll get hot."

"Where's your helmet?" Silly question, considering little could kill him, but little could kill her, too.

"Being useful to someone who needs it." He twisted the throttle on the handlebar. The bike roared and rumbled more. He reached back and grabbed her hip in a gentle, but firm grip. With a sharp tug, she was pressed flush to his back. His hand trailed down her leg to rest on her knee. "Better. Stay close. I don't bite."

"I believe that's the first lie you've spoken to me," she teased.

"I don't bite while driving." Draven flashed her a quick smile in the mirror, fangs and all. "Are you ready?"

Vivian tightened her arms around his chest, her legs hugging close to his. She pressed her body to his back, absorbing the strength in his lean muscles and hard frame. The moon remained hidden behind a thick swell of clouds, and she hoped they would dissipate soon. She had waited all day for this moment. The moment when Draven arrived. When she would learn the truth about them.

She nodded, the bulky helmet making her feel like her head would fall off. She giggled, her heart light and her spirit soaring. Whatever nightmares awaited her, she refused to let them have a place in her thoughts when she was with Draven.

And it seemed to work. Her willpower. Or maybe it was something else entirely. The blackness remained at bay.

He gave her knee a squeeze. Warmth flowed through her leg and settled in her belly.

"Remember, just lean with me."

"Be one with the charmer. Got it."

Something dark and carnal flashed through his eyes. "That could be misinterpreted, love."

She didn't doubt that. The heat that flushed through her at his implication was as potent as the sparks that flamed to life when he touched her.

Draven twisted the throttle and the engine roared. He kicked up the stand and they were off.

At first, Vivian pressed herself hard to Draven, ducking her head as a sickening mixture of fear and exhilaration threatened to make her lose her supper. As the minutes passed, Vivian's muscles unfurled from the grip of tension. She dared to lift her head off Draven's back.

When she did, when she was able to feel the wind on her face and inhale the crisp night air, sheer pleasure encompassed her. The freedom of the road on the back of his motorcycle. The hum of the powerful engine beneath her. The sight of the pavement as they flew over it. The sounds of the night.

She lifted her head, her face, and watched the night sky above the blur of tree branches as they headed out of Nocturne Falls along the two-lane road flanked by thick forest. The thick haze of clouds began to thin as Draven guided the bike with precision, expertise, and a thrilling grace. Her arms loosened and lowered to his stomach, a plane of steely muscle she felt through his thick sweater. She caught his gaze in the mirrors, along with a heart-skipping, handsome grin.

The toe of his boot kicked up on the shifter with a click. The engine rumbled. The bike lurched forward faster than ever.

Vivian laughed.

*Gods, the freedom!*

She would have never considered herself the risky type. She preferred the safety and security of the known, not the unreliability of the unknown.

But tonight?

*I want this forever.*

She lost track of how long they rode. Between the shield of Draven's body and the leather pants that covered her legs and the jacket her arms, the night chill couldn't touch her. They slowed only for turns. She leaned into each one with him, anxious for the next one, loving the sense of danger with each deep tip of the bike. He must have sensed her excitement, and fed her want for more. He dared to go into the turns a little faster, making the dips a little steeper. When they hit patches of dirt, he made the bike fishtail and controlled the machine like an expert horseman kept rein on an unruly horse.

At last, they crested a hill to roll into a makeshift parking lot. Beyond the dirt and gravel, grass and a few trees perched on the overlook. A handful of worn benches were scattered across the ledge.

Below, she could see the dazzling glow of lights and tall buildings, hear the distant sound of music and horns and *life*.

Vivian pulled off her helmet when Draven set the bike on the kickstand and shut off the engine. He raked a hand through wind-blow hair that made him look utterly delectable before dropping his palms to his thighs and twisting to look back at her.

The moment her gaze leveled with his, her heart near stopped.

She had been so absorbed by the thrill of the ride, the nearness of Draven, and the view of the city below that she hadn't realized the moon had escaped the confines of the clouds.

And for the first time, every hope and dream, every secret prayer and whimsical wish, came true as she stared at the one inescapable sign shining in his eyes.

The universe, studded with millions of stars and galaxy spirals and nebulas. Clear as the moonlight shining down on them.

Vivian reached up and traced his brow before leaning forward and pressing her lips to his. The sizzle of their skin touching unleashed a basic and furious hunger that had been locked away inside her.

She slipped her tongue between his lips, leading the way into a kiss that she craved until he took control with a slant of his mouth and a possessive plunder.

His arm snaked around her waist. Her boot slipped from the peg as he pulled her around his body and over his lap, her bottom landing on the hump of the gas tank. A fierce groan rumbled from his chest and resonated through each and every bone in her body.

Oh, the sensations that pummeled her were so alien, yet so delicious and right. They heightened and intensified with every sweep of his tongue, every barely controlled caress of his hands over her back and arms and legs. He encompassed her with his touch, claimed her with his kiss, and unleashed the magic inside her spirit.

She shifted on the gas tank, untangling her legs from the side of the bike to straddle Draven in a far more comfortable position. It took less than a second for her to realize how provocative the position she had settled on was when his hands gripped her waist tightly and he pulled her closer, pressing her back until she lay caged between the tank and the handlebars.

*Oh my.*

Draven's kiss deepened. Vivian sank her hands into his soft hair, keeping him close.

Not that it took much.

Draven began to forge a sensual trail of kisses and nips down her neck. She closed her eyes and sighed beneath the delight, the pleasure, the tingling in her throat and her gums.

His teeth, those fierce fangs, scraped her skin and she moaned, arching into him.

"Sweet hell," he growled, releasing a sharp breath. His hands slipped up her sides beneath her leather jacket until they curled around her shoulders and brought them even closer. "Vivian, what have you done to me?"

The strain in his voice caught her by surprise. He sounded as though the feelings washing over them pained him.

It almost shattered her euphoria—until he lifted his head from placing a kiss in the hollow of her neck and pressed his forehead to hers.

A tender, meaningful motion.

His eyes were so dark, his pupils swallowed up the blue. His face held a faint shade of rose. His nostrils flared as he breathed. Sharp, shallow breaths.

"I don't know what you've done me, but I never want you to stop. I never want us to stop. You haunt me every minute of every day. This...this need drives me crazy." He caught her bottom lip between his own. "Vivian..."

"Say you'll be mine," she whispered, a soft plea that echoed in her heart.

Draven leaned back and stared down at her for an extended moment. He sat up straight and pulled her up, cupping her face in his hands.

"I'm supposed to ask that of you." His thumb traced her upper lip. The corner of his mouth twitched and his lips parted to show the tips of his fangs. Vivian tore her gaze from his mouth, wanting more of his powerful kiss, and stared into the star-studded evidence in his eyes. "Be mine. From now until forever."

She nodded. "You were meant for me."

His hands slipped back into her hair, his fingers curling gently against her scalp. Somehow, her braids had fallen loose without her noticing. He pulled her closer until their noses brushed.

"I hope that's true."

"It is. It's in your eyes. The proof."

Said eyes narrowed.

Vivian tried to smile, but the emotions crashing through her weakened her. The air between them thrummed with heat and electricity too strong to break with a smile. She slipped her fingers around the back of his neck.

"The moon is full and I see every hope and dream, every promise of the future in your eyes. The stars and the universe."

"Something from your fae roots?"

"Yes."

"Like soul mates?"

Vivian finally managed a trembling smile. "That's my understanding. We see the universe in the eyes of the one we're meant for. That's what happened between Kalen and Fawn."

"I don't see it in yours, but your eyes are hypnotic

tonight." He drew a finger along the tip of her pointed ear and slowly trailed that same finger down her face. "Your skin is almost ghostly, but you are…" He gave his head a slight shake. "Beautiful is too weak a word. I have no words to describe you, or what you do to me."

Yes, she was soaring far above the clouds, the world, the stars, realizing that there was at least a small promise of security with Draven. And with the fervor in his next kiss, a potent measure of desperation and possession, she knew deep down he felt that same security and assurance.

One of his hands began to ease beneath her sweater when the crunch of gravel beneath tires pulled them apart. Vivian struggled to catch her breath as they looked toward the narrow road. Headlights grew brighter as a car drew closer to the overlook.

Draven chuckled ruefully, grabbed her waist and lifted her from him and the bike in one easy motion. She smoothed out her hair, fixing it to hide the points of her ears. Showing them off in Nocturne Falls was one thing. Beyond the town limits, her disguise had to go into place.

When she caught the strange way her hand left an ethereal path as it fell from her hair, she quickly stopped Draven from climbing off the bike. He must've seen the worry in her expression, because his brows came together. His lips, red and swollen from their kisses, pulled down at the corners.

He molded a palm against her cheek. "What is it, love?"

Vivian slowly waved her hand in front of him, showing him the ghostly trail of light. "I can't stay here. Not around humans. I can hide my ears, but not this."

He dipped his head slightly. The expression on his face, one of understanding and determination, made the base of her throat tingle. Draven said she was beautiful. He was just as gorgeous.

"Do you want to stay?" he asked.

Vivian cast the path down the mountain a glance. The car was coming closer. "I can't."

"You didn't answer my question. Do you *want* to?"

She pressed her lips together and gazed out over the stunning scene below. It was a sight unlike anything she'd experienced and she certainly had hoped to enjoy more of it.

She gave a small nod.

Draven dragged his thumb down her lips. He climbed off the bike, snagging her bottom lip between his teeth in a quick, playful nip before stretching up to his full, enticing height. Without a word, he shrugged off his jacket and placed it around Vivian's shoulders, turning the collar up.

"Come on. Chances are whoever's coming up here is going to become too busy to notice anything. And I plan on having you tucked against me as we enjoy the view."

# Chapter 14

*"You were meant for me."*

Draven barely took the view in, despite the dazzling lights and the liveliness he could hear all the way up the mountainside. He was too enthralled by Vivian's small frame tucked perfectly against his side, beneath his arm. Each slow beat of her heart managed to somehow thrum in his chest. Each calm breath fed his own lungs air he didn't require. His fingers drew lazy circles over her arm and shoulder as he burned from the touch.

He'd nearly lost himself earlier, and couldn't be more thankful for the car that was parked a few yards from his bike. Although he had called it—the couple inside had already done a fine job fogging up the windows—their presence cooled his body temperature enough to regain control over the intoxicating effects of the woman beside him.

"I've never seen anything so breathtaking in real

life," Vivian murmured. It was the first thing she had said since they took a seat on one of the benches that opened a door into her past. Despite their enjoyable meal the night before, she remained unforthcoming about her past, and what she had shared had been vague and obscure.

"I'll show you anything your heart can dream," he said, leaning down to kiss the top of her head. The implied vow behind his words struck him. He spoke as he had so many times to his sister. Promises he made sure to keep, whatever the cost.

"You've shown me more. You've shown me hope."

Draven shifted to block any sight of Vivian from the car and met her eyes. Those eyes that stole the breathlessness from his lungs.

Stole his heart.

"Why would you say that? Surely you know hope."

A sad almost-smile touched her mouth. "Yes and no. My brother was always my well of hope until something went wrong. Then Fawn and our friends in Nocturne Falls became a new ray of hope. Until recently."

"I don't understand." Something dark and ominous pinched the back of his memory. He narrowed his gaze, curling a lock of her silken hair around his fingers. "The doctor your brother mentioned. And a...lab. Is that what you're talking about?" When her gaze dropped and she sidled closer, tucking her head into his chest, he knew he'd hit the bull's-eye. "Will you tell me about it? Were you sick?"

"No. Not before the lab."

He now understood the sensation of one's gut plummeting. The sickening feeling in his stomach threatened to put a damper on the evening. But he'd learn about Vivian's past. Learn it well so she would never have to worry about it again.

She let out a long breath. "I was two, Kalen five, when we were taken. Our parents were killed. I never met our father, and barely remember our mother. We were the product of a crazy man's desire to make a day-walking vampire. Our parents were captives who escaped. Kalen and I were born while they were in hiding. Jackson's uncle helped them escape, then years later helped us escape. He worked for Dr. Hamstead, but he protected us best he could. He taught us about the outside world through books and movies and magazines. He taught us to read and write, math and the basic elements to survive. To live beyond the walls of the lab and our rooms. Our cells."

Draven's muscles stiffened until his neck ached. He flexed his fingers from her shoulders before his nails tore through the leather and into her skin from the threatening anger.

He had expected secrets. Not a damn nightmare.

There was nothing to indicate she was lying or exaggerating, not that he could imagine her doing so, but…a lab?

*And now the old bones want her dead.*

"Experiments?"

Even as the word rolled from his tongue, it left painful punctures along its path.

She shuddered. "So much worse. The tests they performed were nothing shy of horrendous. My skin has healed, but the places they would biopsy and peel and puncture...I still feel every poke and prod."

"Did anyone ever..." His throat tightened as his rage swelled. "Did anyone dare..."

Against his chest, he felt her head move. A shake.

Thank the heavens.

But at the same moment, he realized the innocence he'd always seen in her was true innocence. Her life must have taught her horrors and provided wisdom someone of her age should never comprehend, but she had yet to learn or experience the joys, right down to intimacy.

"Kalen made his threats and Nicholas, Jackson's uncle, wouldn't allow anyone to do anything to compromise me." A ripple of nervousness rolled off her. "I hope you're not disappointed."

He swallowed back his shame. To think he'd been about to ravage her on his bike. Nope. Not happening. She deserved a bed of rose petals and candlelight and tenderness. Not the hungry beast clawing inside him to get out.

"I am certainly not disappointed. How could I be?"

She shrugged. "Kalen doesn't know the extent of the tests they performed on me."

She lifted her head, her eyes sad and her face drawn. Gods, she looked like an angel. A sad angel. It tore into his heart.

"Please don't tell him. If he ever found out how

horrendous the tests were, he'd never forgive himself. He's dedicated his life to me and keeping me safe."

"I won't discuss this with him. It's between us." He could only imagine how he'd feel if Sophia confided in another and swore him to secrecy. It would kill him inside. The bond between Vivian and Kalen, he believed, ran deeper than his and Sophia's. Then again, their bond was something a nightmare forged to keep hope alive. No amount of antiquity, whether it be rules or a way of life, could compare to what he only imagined Vivian suffered. "There's something else. Something I've sensed bothering you. The reason you hid from me yesterday?"

There was a long, tumultuous silence. He could almost feel the storm of her thoughts pounding inside his own head.

"Dr. Hamstead's last experiment. He injected me with what Jackson has deemed a virus that created a monster. It slowly ate away at my conscience, the fae in me. It called to the vampire, but the beast of a vampire. Nothing like you or the others I've met. The doctor ordered my termination because his experiment went wrong. That's when Nicholas helped us escape the lab. He was murdered while on the run, but instructed us to come to Nocturne Falls and to his nephew for a cure."

She reached for his hand, and only then did he realize his fingers had curled so tight she had to pry him off her. Her touch, as gentle as it was, soothed the fury seething beneath his skin. The touch of her lips against his fingertips eased the muscles along his back.

"He found one, I'm guessing. I've yet to see a monster in you."

"Actually, Hugh Ellingham, one of the men who helps run Nocturne Falls, came up with something. We thought it worked."

*Oh, damn.*

"You *thought*?"

She took a sharp breath and pushed off him, flashing him a smile that tried to make him forget what she was talking about. It failed.

Failed miserably because he knew now that he had to keep Garrett away from her after he practically led the coven leader right to her.

Draven held onto her hand. "Vivian, the virus was eradicated, wasn't it?"

The dip of her head said enough. As did the unease in his gut. She was still sick with whatever the doctor put inside her body.

"I swear, if I get my hands on this guy—"

"He's behind bars. He won't be coming out."

Draven scowled. "Got off easy, in my opinion." He grabbed her other hand and kissed the knuckles of both. "Well, since you've confided that we're meant for each other, I can officially say you're stuck with me. I'm not going anywhere, so no more hiding and making me ask your brother for help finding you. So, what do we do to fix this problem?"

Her eyes sparkled, and this time, he smelled the salt in her tears. Her smile quivered.

"I don't know. They're working it out. Jackson and

Hugh. They're trying to figure out how to get rid of it for good. Hugh is running some comparative tests while he tweaks the last antidote and Jackson's keeping track of the virus's progress through blood work and monitoring. He knows my symptoms, what to look for. Just…bear with me."

Perhaps that was the suspicion and unease he sensed in the man at the house. Perhaps it was because of Jackson's dedication toward Vivian and not necessarily male yearning for a beautiful woman.

And here he thought *his* life was pitiful at times.

The Fates had dropped him dead center into this proverbial hell to save a woman who stole pieces of his heart faster than he could stop her. Not that he wanted to. And he would do whatever it took to make sure she stayed safe.

Draven pressed his forehead to hers. "Vivian, I'll be your rock. You can lean on me whenever you need to. You can scream and shout and punch and kick in frustration. I'm not going anywhere." He kissed her, a chaste, lingering kiss. "Nowhere."

The night grew cold as the hours passed. It wasn't until the car left that Draven suggested they head back to Nocturne Falls. It was nearing midnight. He managed to turn the dismal mood around as they'd talked, and thoroughly loved the sound of her sweet laughter as he shared the rather embarrassing adventures from his first trips into the modern world after a few decades in the dark.

"How do you feel about going to a club? Saturday night, still early, and I hear Insomnia is supposed to be a hit," Draven said, throwing his leg over the bike and settling onto his seat. He swallowed down the lump that bobbed up into his throat at the vivid memory of seeing Vivian spread, lush and inviting, over the bike's gas tank. Yeah, she was definitely becoming his addiction. "If you're not tired."

Vivian flashed him one of her sexy smiles, the one that struck him dead center through the chest, wrapped hot coils around his unbeating heart and breathed life into his body. He couldn't get over the ghostly appearance of her skin when the moonlight hit her, or how bright her eyes grew as the night wore on. An alluring magic, a sensual and magnetic power, rolled through her spirit, something he sensed but didn't understand. He chalked it up to her fae blood, which he had yet to learn the details of.

She veered away from that topic as smoothly as her brother had the other night. He couldn't begin to fathom why.

She climbed onto the bike behind him, her knees tucked under his thighs. She slipped her arms beneath his jacket, locking her hands against his stomach. He glanced back when she rested her chin on his shoulder and gave him that dazzling smile.

"Are you sure I can trust you in a dark club?"

Aww, geez. Her playful jabs prodded his control.

"No more than you can trust me on an overlook."

"Then Insomnia it is."

He shifted in the saddle and started the bike. It roared to life as he twisted the throttle and kicked up the stand.

"No helmet?" he asked.

"I'd like to feel the wind on my face and enjoy the thrill of the ride."

A woman after his own heart, for sure.

"Very well, then, love."

He spun out the back tire, sending an arc of pebbles and dirt into the air. Vivian laughed, body pressed to his as he sent the bike barreling down the mountain road. Her excitement shone like a bright light inside him and he wanted nothing more than to feed her joy. She rode passenger perfectly, moving with him and the bike around curves and turns. When the road opened up, he pushed the bike to risky speeds. Every few minutes, he stole a glance at Vivian in his mirrors, his own smile reflecting her carefree expression. Her hair blew like a silken cape behind her and when she tipped her head to look up at the sky, his gums ached as bad as his lips to claim her neck.

They reached the two-lane road leading into Nocturne Falls, and he goosed the throttle, switched gears with the toe of his boot, and punched forward.

He had no time to avoid the creature that appeared in the road.

Vivian shrieked.

He jerked the handlebars.

The bike hit an invisible ramp even as the tires squealed and lost traction, launching off the ground and into the air.

Draven cussed aloud, contorting his body to wrap around Vivian's small frame as she flailed in the air. He used the pegs to launch off the airborne bike, twisting with Vivian burrowed against his chest and encased within his arms.

When he hit the ground, landing on his feet, he caught a split-second flash of his bike hovering upside down far above their heads.

Vivian was ripped out of his embrace.

A force he couldn't see, but sure as hell felt, slammed into his midsection, sending him flying backward to smack into the unforgiving pavement.

Gray obscured his vision.

When he tried to sit up, his limbs refused to obey his commands. His arms and legs were held stuck to the ground by an unknown force. His fingers moved and he could only lift his head enough to see Vivian fighting the figure's embrace, reaching a free arm toward him.

"Vivia—" he bellowed, only to have his voice cut off with some kind of stricture around his throat.

The creature removed the hood from its head.

His head.

A head that looked awfully similar to Vivian's. Ghostly white hair with a strange golden circlet set low on his head. Eyes so light a blue they were almost silver. Those eyes pierced him with a chilling electrical shock that jerked Draven's muscles.

He looked incorporeal. Draven swore he could see the street through the creature's fluttering pants and rippling cloak. His hair floated around his shoulders, giving him the appearance of being submerged in transparent liquid.

"Do not fight, child. You are one of us."

The voice was as hollow and ghostly as the rest of him, and carried on the air all around them. Draven doubted he spoke to anyone but Vivian.

Vivian's back went stiff, her eyes wide. She spun away from Draven, and he could only imagine the look on her face. Her fight ceased.

Draven tried to call out to her again, but his voice failed. He fought the invisible bindings pinning him to the ground, to no avail.

Suddenly, a whoosh of air shot over him. He swore the ground beneath him rippled. His head bounced off the pavement. The bike, which had been suspended upside down in the air, flipped over and dropped onto its tires before falling with a cringe-worthy thunk-thud-crunch to the ground.

Another strange ripple of air rushed at him.

His bike vanished.

Gone.

Draven's body tore off the ground and he became airborne again. The sensation of flying weightlessly didn't last more than a second. Nor did his view of the forest and street and strange astral creature glowing in the moonlight.

He blinked.

His feet hit the ground. He stumbled as he fought off the disorientation from weightlessness.

For a long moment, he stared at his surroundings, beyond confused.

Darkness, except for the faintest shimmer of light from the moon. Oh, the familiar smells of dirt and must mixed in with hints of his cologne assaulted him.

A door opened. Blue eyes widened in the darkness. "Draven?"

*Sophia?*

A flash, followed by a loud crash shattered the otherwise solid silence, reverberating through the floor. The sliver of moonlight that escaped the closed curtains glinted off pieces of metal and chrome that had come away from his carelessly deposited motorcycle.

Smack dab in the middle of his bedchamber at Levoire Mansion.

Sweet gods, what the hell just *happened*?

# Chapter 15

"Where did he go?" Vivian yelled.

The fae released his hold on her wrist at last. Vivian took off down the eerily quiet road to where Draven had been only moments ago, the click of her heels on the pavement the only sound in the night. Panic speared through her mind, her body reacting with a fierce rush of urgency.

"What did you do to him?" she demanded.

There was no evidence of Draven on the pavement. Nothing. Not even a residual scent of his cologne or marks from the bike.

Nothing. It was as if he never existed.

The being appeared in front of her. She spun away, desperate to find a clue as to what had happened to Draven. Every direction she twisted or ran, the fae appeared to block her.

"He is not of consequence, child. Cease your search."

That airy, almost hollow voice chilled her to the marrow. She had to fight down the shudder that threatened to conquer her body.

When she failed in one more attempt to escape, she stamped her booted foot on the ground and faced the creature, anger and fear warring inside her.

"Not of consequence? How do you know such things?" she snapped. A lifetime of facing daily nightmares forged a bit of a backbone, even if she preferred to avoid conflict. But this new strength that unfurled throughout her spirit and seized control was rooted in her violent separation from Draven. "Who are you?"

"We are all."

She narrowed her gaze. "You are *nothing*." She crossed her arms over her chest in a show of defiance when the man's incorporeal face appeared to harden at her insult. "Why are you here?"

"To bring you and Kalen home."

Her eyes widened. "Home?" She shook her head. "We *are* home."

The fae's expression rippled and softened, as did the light in his eyes. "No, child. This is not your home. You belong with us."

Vivian played his logic in her head. Based on the very little she knew of her ancestry and the Celestial fae, she had an inkling these beings didn't take no for an answer. They were perceived as far more powerful than other breeds of fae. A haughty essence rolled off this man, one that reinforced her suspicion that he believed himself far above anyone not of his breeding.

In his mind, he was superior to all.

He provided her first taste of disgust for her Celestial blood. She never recalled her mother being so…arrogant.

No, every memory of her mother was of a beautiful woman who loved and cared to a fault. It was more a strong impression that remained with her than an actual memory.

"Kalen won't leave. And neither will I. This is our home. It has been for the entirety of our lives," Vivian finally said, the sharp edge in her voice faltering. "He has found his soul mate." She glanced toward the empty space on the street where she had last seen Draven. "And so have I."

"'Tis nonsense you speak." He held out an imperious hand. "Come with me. Let me show you home."

Vivian shook her head. "I'm not leaving here. Not without Kalen. He won't leave Fawn, and I refuse to leave Draven." She leveled her gaze on the man. "You chose now to come to us. After all these years in captivity, suffering as experiments. After our mother and father were murdered. Why are you only now making an appearance? Just when we are getting our lives in order, you want to destroy this small gift of peace."

The man tilted his head in a way that told her he didn't understand what she spoke of. She took a step back. He didn't follow, only observed her with that tinge of incomprehension. Did he believe he was so superior that these simple ideas didn't register?

"Where's Draven?" she asked. "What did you do to him?"

"He is where he belongs, child. He is not of consequence, and he is certainly not this soul mate you speak of. We choose our mates. Our *equals*."

His words confirmed his thought process. He didn't realize mates were chosen for them, not the other way around. Her own mother embraced that. It was Vivian's mother who told her about seeing the universe in the eyes of a soul mate.

Kalen couldn't be certain that their parents were soul mates, but she held little doubt in her heart.

"I believe our definition of equal is far different," she said. "Bring Draven back to me."

The man gave a single shake of his head. His presence alone somehow swept calm over her, draining her of the fight.

"No. He is not deserving of a place by your side."

"Then I want to go back to Kalen." Together, they'd figure this out, whatever it was that needed figuring out.

The fae touched two fingers to her forehead. A split second later, she rocked on her feet inside Fawn's small cottage.

Kalen burst out of the bedroom, his expression fierce and his body tense, dressed in only a pair of night pants, hair mussed. She sheepishly looked way. Gods, she hated interrupting her brother's time with Fawn. And

Fawn's delay in arriving in the hallway assured Vivian she'd interrupted something pretty sweet.

The fae lifted his hand toward Fawn.

Kalen immediately placed himself between his soul mate and the unknown fae. "Who are you?" His sharp gaze cut to Vivian before returning to their latest threat. "Vivian, are you okay?"

"No. He did something to Draven. Made him disappear," Vivian said without hesitation, giving the fae a wide berth as she hurried to Kalen's side. She found strength in her brother's nearness, but her body also acted as another shield to protect Fawn. "He won't tell me who he is."

"Celestial fae," Kalen said, stating the obvious. "If I'm to guess, High Guard. One of the royals. What house are you from?"

For the first time, the fae appeared to acknowledge another royal. He gave a small bow of his head. "House of N'Agra. The crown of Xyna has awoken after silence for many decades. I would like to inquire about Mauryn."

"I was under the impression the Celestial fae were all-knowing."

The man gave them a thin smile. His hazy appearance became more corporeal before Vivian's eyes. The unfelt breeze that seemed to touch him alone ceased, his hair settling in a glowing white fall around his shoulders. His clothing became detailed, from the stitching and style to the vibrant colors of gold and ivory.

"Of the universe, but not to those of our equal."

"Then how do you know of us?" Vivian asked. She felt Kalen's quick side glance.

"You've been tainted by something not of our fae blood."

Tainted.

Mr. House of N'Agra spoke the word sympathetically, if that were even possible for a being of his lofty breeding. Vivian found it interesting that he might understand sympathy, but not feel a bond as strong as that between soul mates.

"Um, excuse me." Fawn pushed her way between Vivian and Kalen and cleared her throat. Vivian grabbed her wrist and gave a small shake of her head. Fawn patted her hand. "It's okay." To the fae, she said, "Can you bring Draven back? He's been handling another issue surrounding Kalen and Vivian."

"The vampires?" the man asked with a scowl.

"Apparently, from our father's side of the family," Kalen said.

Vivian understood why Kalen gave the being who thought everyone several classes below his standing this information. For one, Vivian was curious to see how this man would react to hearing of their mixed — wait, *tainted* — blood. Second, maybe their tainted blood would make him leave in disgust.

She was beginning to despise this side of her family, if he was somehow related to them. Especially when his lips curled down in a scowl. She could only hope her father's family was more inviting.

Kalen gave Fawn's arm a firm tug, forcing her back behind the wall of their bodies. Vivian heard the elf's put-out huff and managed a small grin.

If there was one thing she and Kalen had over Fawn, it was experience dealing with unreasonable monsters. This one was no exception.

"Mauryn would never lower herself to mate with a parasite," N'Agra groused.

Kalen scowled back, this time showing with two extended fangs the evidence that apparently their mother *had* so lowered herself, at least in the eyes of her Celestial kin. "She never lowered herself. She loved, and received our father's love in return. He protected her, sacrificed himself for her, when her own people abandoned her."

"She had been lost—"

"Not to the all-knowing. She had her crown. You could've traced her, right? You could have found her, but you turned your backs on her when she needed your help. Ignored the children she bore."

Vivian stepped forward quickly, her leg blocking Kalen's when he took a step toward the fae.

"Vivi…"

"Wait." Vivian moved up to the man and watched him closely. Stared him straight in the eyes and somehow read what he was hiding deep inside. "How are you related to us? And what is your name?"

The name he gave was in another language, their native Celestial tongue. It was a sound more than a word, a lilt of his tongue and fluid song of his vocal cords. He did not possess a name that translated into a language for others to understand. She recognized the ancient tune as it called to her spirit.

"Cerryan," he added. "For name's sake. Such as Mauryn." He produced another song of sound, and she realized he was sharing their mother's name in that same ancient tongue. "Our language cannot be defined beyond our realm. There is no translation."

"And our kinship?"

"'Tis complicated and inconsequential at this time."

"No, I believe it *is* consequential. We are the last of our bloodline. Kalen succeeds our mother's place in our House."

"All the more reason to return to our realm." Cerryan's clear blue eyes lifted from Vivian and hung on Kalen. "Should you resume your place as the next royal of the House of Xyna, you will forfeit your...life here. If you choose not to comply, your crown will be distributed to a new House royal and your ties cut to us."

"Well, isn't that cheeky," Fawn muttered.

"I don't think there's much that needs to be discussed or weighed in that decision," Kalen said. "We've learned more about our vampire line than our Celestial line over the course of our lives."

"Do not be deceived by the vampires, son of Mauryn. They hold no honor in their ways and will see you dead."

Vivian gasped, the feeling of being punched in the stomach rendering her breathless. Certainly, that wasn't true. Why would they want her and Kalen dead?

Cerryan's expression grew blank, his eyes cold. He held out his hand. "I shall request the crown of Xyna."

"It's not here," Fawn interjected, her voice steady and hard. "We don't keep it here for security purposes."

A faint chill rode up Vivian's spine. Something wasn't right with his request. He was able to determine that the crown had awoken recently. He traced the energy here. He should know the crown's location.

"I have an idea," Vivian said, flashing her frustrated brother a bright smile. "Why don't we meet tomorrow night? That way, Kalen and I can discuss this when temperaments have calmed." She faced Cerryan. "Would you agree to that?"

His gaze chilled her worse that the expression on his face. His ethereal form began to take over his more solid form.

"We do not negotiate—"

The air around them pulsed, knocking Vivian off balance. The electric bolt that zipped through the sizzling air was unforgiving, making her skin burn and her heart sputter.

The cottage vanished in a blink.

And the desolate road leading into Nocturne Falls appeared.

Only instead of standing alone with Cerryan after he made Draven disappear, she stood in the center of the road with Kalen, Fawn, and a stunned Draven, who clutched a young woman against him.

An instant later, another woman blinked into being out of thin air, her appearance as ethereally insubstantial as Cerryan's. A rush of urgency surrounded her as she grabbed Vivian's hand.

"I must get you away from here before he returns."

Before Vivian could take another breath, the scene disappeared again.

When her feet connected with solid ground once more, she found herself in the center of a strange, opulent room that shimmered in a nighttime glow beneath thousands and thousands of stars. Distant galaxies.

And the moon, a bright, silver orb, was the focus of this alternate universe.

"Where the heck are we now?"

Vivian spun at the sound of Draven's irritated voice. He quickstepped to her side, pulling her into his chest with one arm while his other held the young woman protectively close.

The Celestial woman appeared before them. A frown pinched her mouth and creased her forehead.

"I have brought you to the only place I know is safe." She spread her arms. "Welcome to my home."

# Chapter 16

"And who are you?" Kalen asked. There was not a hint of kindness in his tone. He wasted no time demanding an introduction from this stranger who poofed into his bedchamber before anyone in Levoire Mansion responded to the sound of his bike crashing to the floor. Sophia jumped into his arms and he had barely embraced her to shield her from this newest threat before his body went through an upsetting transport it had experienced less than a minute before.

Gods, his head was spinning.

And now, Vivian tucked against him on one side, his sister wrapped in his jacket to protect her skin and eyes tucked on the other side, he damn well wanted to know what the hell was going on.

The woman appeared to float more than walk, even if she looked solid and not ghostly like the man who magically shooed him back home. She stepped into the center of their little horseshoe-shaped half-circle and lowered her head in a small bow. "Call me as you please."

"A name," Kalen demanded.

The woman lifted her head, her expression serene. "Call me…Nalia."

Draven suppressed a gasp when the woman turned her attention on him. She was beautiful, with pale blond hair and eyes that shone so clear they seemed almost translucent. Had it not been for the specks of gold, he might have questioned her ability to see.

Nalia reached for the jacket secured around Sophia. "She is safe in this light, this realm, I assure you. Her ailments are products of Earth, not of the stars."

Vivian leaned back. The small distance injected a new coolness inside him, one he didn't like and wanted to cast away.

"Sophia?" his goddess asked before turning her questioning gaze to him.

Draven opened his mouth to answer, but his attention jerked back to Sophia as Nalia slowly peeled the jacket away from her. His first instinct was to shove the strange fae woman away, but as she exposed Sophia's flawless pale skin and fear-filled eyes, shock rattled his nerves. She remained unharmed.

It had been so long since he'd last seen his sister in light, decades, and she had been the equivalent of an adolescent at that time. A time before anything except candlelight and darkness became her drab world.

"What ailments?" Fawn asked, drawing close to Draven and Vivian, Kalen less than half a step behind her. Sophia tucked her face into his chest, her black hair falling over her cheek. "Who is she?"

"My sister," Draven said. He sighed, giving Sophia's shoulder a squeeze. "Love, it's okay."

His gaze brushed over Vivian when he spoke the endearment. For some reason, it didn't feel the same on his tongue now. Not when spoken to his sister. That endearment belonged to the woman who stepped back to give him enough room to gently pry Sophia away from him.

Nalia held a hand close to Sophia's exposed skin. Light formed a baseball-sized orb and danced in her palm. It twinkled like she had captured a million stars in the small globe.

"She suffers no harm." Nalia twirled a finger from her other hand through the orb, dismissing the light. "The sunlight cannot harm this young woman here, nor can any light that may cause her harm on Earth."

She lowered her arms to her sides, her smile serene.

With that, Draven connected the similarities between this strange woman and Vivian. It wasn't so much their looks as it was the essence of their power. The thrum of calm and peace.

Nalia nodded once, the motion slow and calculated. "It is an essence that resonates through each of us."

"You can read my mind," Draven said. He shot Vivian a guarded glance. Her expression reflected his shock. She inched closer to Draven, her hand clasped tightly with his.

"That is a complicated assumption, with an equally complicated answer," Nalia said.

"Draven, the small talk can wait," Kalen interrupted, edging between Nalia and the group. Had Draven not had his own sister clinging to him for dear life, he would have taken offense by Kalen assuming command of the situation. "I believe you should be answering questions pertaining to the events this evening. Where we are. And why."

Nalia gave Kalen an approving nod. "You have Mauryn's selflessness and drive for goodness within you. And Vivian, your heart resonates with your beloved mother's peace and purity. You two are your mother's children."

She manifested over one hand a gold circlet with strange gems shimmering within the elegant gold lacework.

"Wait, where did you—"

"It must be protected," Nalia said, cutting into Fawn's shocked exclamation.

"Okay, hold up a minute, because I'm getting the feeling I'm missing something." Draven shot Kalen an icy look before giving Vivian a much softer look. He pointed to the circlet. "I'm not going to pretend to be an expert on fae and their breeds and such, but it doesn't take a know-all to guess what that is."

"A crown," Nalia confirmed, but his attention was on Vivian.

Her eyelids dropped, followed by her head. He caught the shift of her jaw as she chewed her lip.

"Vivian?" Why did that sinking feeling in his gut have to return now? Oh, right. Crown. "What's going on? And who is she?" He motioned to Nalia with a flick of his hand. "Where are we?"

"I don't know where we are. I've never been here before. And I'm not sure who Nalia is."

"Mauryn was my sister," Nalia offered.

The silence that followed could steal a person's hearing, it was so loud. Draven caught the cacophony of beating hearts as they up-ticked in pace. The looks that passed between everyone could redefine the meaning of shock.

None of it helped clear up what was going on. How Sophia seemed immune in this place to the dangers that would on Earth have either killed her or left her severely crippled. There was no sun here, at least for the moment, but Draven wasn't about to take this stranger's word that a hearty dose of UV tonic would prove harmless.

*All this time, I thought living with the Levoire coven was an episode of The Twilight Zone. And now this.*

He reeled under this latest wrench in life. It took a few breaths to realize the reeling sensation didn't come from him. It resonated from Vivian. He *felt* her turmoil like it was his own. A dark, bubbling pit of hesitation, anticipation, caution, and so much more.

"How did you find the circlet?" Kalen asked, the command in his tone gone. He took the object when Nalia held it out to him.

"How did you get to it before Cerryan? And why

give it back to Kalen if we are to forfeit our right to our mother's bloodline?" Vivian pressed.

"You are *not* to forfeit your title as High Guard. Cerryan has waited centuries for the opportunity to obtain royal status—"

"*Royal*?" Draven couldn't help that the word sounded more like a bark than an inquiry. The news smacked his thoughts. His eyes went wide as he looked at Vivian. His woman, who claimed they were meant for one another, was royalty. Royalty! The closest to royal he'd ever been was royally screwed. Like right now. "You're kidding."

"Kalen and Vivian are descendants of a very renowned and highly respected house of the High Guard. Our council anxiously awaited their return until it became clear they were not meant to return to the stars. Their place is on Earth, to create a new liaison between the many races of beings and ourselves." Nalia turned her beatific smile on Kalen. "It is why we have not sought you out. Not until Cerryan interfered this evening. Do not ever hand your crown to another, Kalen. Your power comes from the stone during the full moon, as it does for all Celestial fae."

Sophia's head jerked up and her eyes narrowed on Nalia, then on Kalen and Vivian. Draven wasn't sure what the big deal was—things didn't get much more big deal-ish beyond being royal—but his sister seemed to realize some significance in this small piece of information.

"But you're legends. Not real," Sophia murmured.

"What do you know about them?" Draven asked, piqued by his sister's knowledge and her hyper-focused attention on Nalia.

"I know that Celestial fae are believed to be god-like in nature. They do not reside on Earth, but dwell throughout the universe," Sophia said, awe in her tone, her eyes hazy. "I have little else to do than read by candlelight. The coven's library holds some ancient books of lore. Fae species were detailed in one of the tomes, and it mentioned Celestial fae. There wasn't much information. The Celestials are elusive. They do not make themselves known unless there is a very good reason."

Fascination and satisfaction crossed Nalia's expression. "You impress me, child, as you are correct."

"And this reason is Cerryan and his attempt to relieve me of my mother's crown," Kalen surmised. "Why didn't he simply call it to him with magic like you did?"

"He cannot sense it. He does not possess a direct connection to the crown, as one of the blood does. He knows there was a ripple of energy from the crown after you placed it on your head to save your soul mate, but he cannot detect its location. He is not the owner of the crown, nor is he a relative of the owner. Our relationship allowed me to locate the crown before Cerryan could. He cannot have the crown, but he'd go to very dangerous lengths to get it."

"I think we're better off with the vampires. I doubt his claim that they'll destroy us is true," Kalen muttered.

Nalia's eyes sparkled. "Oh, no, Kalen. They *will* do that. Destroy you and Vivian." All humor disappeared as quickly as Draven had seen Nalia appear at the mansion. "Your father's coven is not tolerant of outsiders, and anyone who may pose a threat to their way of life will be destroyed. Including you both."

The nonchalance of her tone didn't match the threat in her words. Nor did it help Draven's peace of mind when her shimmering eyes slid to him.

"Ask Draven. He's aware of their plan."

Vivian spun to face him at the same time she wrenched herself from his hold and jumped back. Away from him. That motion left the hooks she had in his heart ripping through the muscle.

"You?" Vivian said on a gasp. "You knew what their plan was all along?"

"Draven." Kalen couldn't sound more lethal if he tried.

Draven threw his hands up in surrender, his attention sweeping over everyone to land on Vivian.

The only person in this alternate realm who seemed at ease and not ready to throttle him was Nalia. And his own sister, of course.

He scowled at the notion, but his internal battle was lost when he caught the pain in Vivian's eyes. The betrayal. All that he cared about was having her listen, hear him out. "I didn't know, I swear it. They arrived last night. Disclosed their plan. They never intended to bring you into the family. They aren't interested in a liaison. They don't want Salvatore's offspring to pose a threat to the laws they've implemented. Laws that include no succession of another coven leader if a blood relative is alive to succeed in proper order." He frowned. "Kalen and you, Vivian."

"Sweet heaven, is there anyone who doesn't want us dead?" Kalen hissed.

The hypnotic, lulling sound of Nalia's laugh was as soft as a breeze yet as full and encompassing as a cloud. "Oh, my sweet nephew. Not everyone wants you dead. I certainly do not, and neither do the rest of the leaders of the royal houses. Cerryan was scorned by your mother, and that is where his animosity remains rooted."

"For an elite being, Nalia, you have a very down-to-Earth manner," Fawn said carefully.

Draven didn't have experience with elite beings, but he found some basis for her claim. Her language was modern, relatable. She wasn't as high-strung as Draven would imagine of someone from an elite race. She certainly didn't hold the stuffiness of the members of the Levoire coven.

Nalia performed some sort of magic that left her hair coiling around her shoulders, her eyes bright beacons of glowing gold light, and her skin shimmering like it was covered in glitter. Draven squinted against the assaulting brightness until Sophia jerked upright with a sharp gasp.

The glow ceased and Nalia returned to her normal—if there was a normal for the fae—self and raised a brow. A calm smile tilted her lips as she looked between Sophia and an equally stunned Fawn.

"You're one of the drawings!" Sophia squeaked.

"In the book Willa lent me," Fawn added. "Someone sketched you."

"Mauryn and I have always held a special curiosity for Earth and Her creations. We spent much time on your plane." Sadness crept into her expression. "Mauryn saved me the night she was captured. We were playing in one of the forests with the animals. Oh, how we loved the deer and the rabbits. We were ambushed. Mauryn used her power to remove me from the plane. I later learned that our presence in that forest was considered trespassing."

"But you never tried to save her?" Vivian asked.

"I imagine it would be difficult for you to understand, Vivian, but we do not interfere with the Fates if we can avoid it. Our station in this existence, as well as our powers, can rival their pathways for the living. And our own. We can alter the course of actions"—her eyes shifted to Kalen—"but our actions have consequences. Your shift in time to save Faunalyn created a disturbance along another path in your life, Kalen, as evidenced by Cerryan's arrival and the Levoire Elders' hunt. There is no blame laid, but you must be instructed in our ways and the power both you and Vivian have."

"She was your sister," Kalen groused.

Sympathy welled deep inside Draven's mind. And he thought his family and living arrangement was dysfunctional.

Instinctively, he reached for Vivian's hand, pleased when her fingers slipped between his and clung for support. The fine creases of her forehead deepened as her eyes shadowed over with a storm of emotions he couldn't begin to dissect. All he knew was he wanted to wash every piece of negativity away from her life.

"And I have suffered grief unlike that which you know." Nalia's voice sounded weighted with that grief. Her admission hung on the air until her concern turned to Vivian. "Had I saved her, you and your brother would never be. The hope for all of Earth beneath the powers of creatures they only believed to be lore and myths would be at risk. She knew this and willingly sacrificed herself to save her children, and do humanity one of the greatest favors. Keep them safe from the unknown. There will be difficult times ahead, and they will need the alliance they will create with us through you."

"Are you all-seeing? All-knowing?" Sophia asked quietly.

"Child, that is a very complicated question. In essence, yes. But like all things powerful, we have our limitations. Our boundaries. Otherwise, the balance of the realms and the universe tips unfavorably." Nalia moved closer to Draven and touched the tip of her finger to his chest. "What I see of you is less than to be desired."

Vivian tried to push between him and Nalia, but the older fae tsked.

"He's my soul mate," Vivian snapped. "And he is *more* than desirable."

Draven grinned, unwinding their hands to wrap his arm around her waist. She held his wrist possessively, and he reveled in the gesture.

"And his life will be forfeit."

In that moment, Draven realized that even the undead could feel the breath of Death against the back of their necks. There was no other way to explain the chill that consumed him, or the darkness that suddenly plagued any promise of a future for him with Vivian.

# Chapter 17

Vivian tried desperately to piece together the shattered bits of her heart, soul, and hope after Nalia suggested they part for rest. Each of them had their own space, small, albeit luxurious rooms surrounded by glass walls and floors and ceilings. They were embraced by the universe, the magic and power vibrating through every cell. The sensation of free-floating alone far beyond Nalia's residence left her aching to find Draven.

The magic in this place was astounding, proof of how easily it flowed in the simplest of things. This room, which she instinctively knew was a wall away from where Draven rested, though there seemed to be no solid walls to divide them. Even the door was made of glass. The illusions were breathtaking, the strength and force apparent in the unbreakable glass while it symbolized the fragility of existence.

Nalia's prophetic words were a dagger in the center of Vivian's crystal world. A dagger that pierced her precious dreams, created a million spider web cracks along the surface until they connected and everything crumbled.

Every action had a consequence.

Kalen saved his soul mate with their powers and, in essence, sentenced Vivian's soul mate to death.

The wail that fled her lips sucked the life from her spirit. She collapsed to her knees and cried into her hands.

"You have a strength inside you that my sister possessed until she took her last breath."

Vivian startled. Nalia knelt beside her and captured her face in warm hands. She wiped the tears from Vivian's face with a sad smile.

"You embody her in every way, Vivian. She would be so proud to see how you've grown. Your suffering granted you wisdom and empathy. You understand pain and loss, and embrace gratitude. Kalen feels the need to protect you, and that is what he's learned. His valiant ways. A symbol of loyalty and love and unwavering determination to do what is right. Neither of you are weak, and tears are by no means a weakness."

She leaned close and pressed a kiss to Vivian's forehead.

"What will happen to Draven?" she asked through quivering lips.

"You cannot stop it, Vivian."

"I'm going to lose him? When I've only just found him? When will everyone I love stop suffering?"

Nalia's lips lifted in a loving smile when Vivian realized the fullness of what she disclosed.

"You do love him." She stroked Vivian's hair, tucking strands behind the points of her ears. "You have not exchanged blood with him. Why? He keeps the poison away."

Vivian blinked. "But..." Oh, the weakness that swept through her. She never felt the virus when Draven was near. She thought it was from the excitement she felt just being close to him. Was there truly more? Was he...could he... "My cure?"

"What I can say, my niece, is that it will not hurt to share. He came to you now. During a time when you believed there was no hope. Never lose hope, sweetness, because you *are* hope. It's your gift."

Nalia swept her fingers over Vivian's eyes, forcing them closed as the moisture was brushed away.

When she opened her eyes, Nalia was gone.

"Love."

Vivian sprung to her feet and turned as Draven strode to her. She had no time to wrap her mind around how he was in her room before his hands were on her face and his mouth crushed down over hers. Her soul sang with joy and sorrow. She sobbed with a rush of happiness and grief.

Draven. She was going to lose Draven.

His hands dropped to her waist and he tugged her flush against him. She clung to his neck, her arms locked in place, fingers fisted in his hair as he lifted her feet from the floor.

"Love," he breathed into her mouth, giving her a small reprieve from drowning in his desire before he consumed her with another powerful, possessive kiss.

The tips of his fangs pricked her lip and tongue with each desperate, hard kiss. Beads of blood rose from the superficial wounds and she drank in the essence of her blood drawn from his passion. The faint shivers that cascaded over his body and the feral growls that bubbled up from his chest were erotic and satisfying. He washed away the weight of their dismal future with each caress of his hands and whisper of adoration.

When his mouth trailed down her neck, she tipped her head, exposing the length of skin over her pulsing vein. "Drink."

Draven scraped his fangs over her flesh. She moaned with a fierce shudder of delight. "Goddess of mine. Light in my darkness. Life to my death."

He sank his fangs deep into her neck.

Vivian gasped, her fingers tightening in his ruffled hair as her legs wrapped desperately around his waist. He hissed against her skin.

Then he drew on her vein, leisurely drinking her essence into his soul, and she melted a hundred times over. He brushed his fingers over her cheek as he continued to drink. She untangled one of her hands from his hair as a deft pulse and tingle crossed through her gums. Her eyes opened to slits, but it was enough to catch the thread of blue beneath the pale skin of his uplifted wrist.

Instinct drove her when she angled his wrist across her mouth and traced her tongue over the tendons. A whisper of heat, those veins.

A deep rumble resonated from Draven's chest right before she tested her aim and bit into his wrist.

Her back hit one of the glass walls as blood splashed over her tongue.

A moan fled her.

A fierce tremor conquered Draven and echoed along her limbs.

Oh, the taste of his essence was brutally dark and delicious. Spicy and powerful. Intoxicating. She lost herself in everything Draven. Potent. Consuming.

"Stop, love."

Draven panted the weak command.

His wrist tugged away from her mouth, only to be replaced by his hungry lips.

The kiss ended far too soon, but when it did, a spark of clarity lit in her fogged head.

She was on her back, on a bed with Draven trembling over her, his eyes black except for a thin, bright blue ring around his pupils. His nostrils flared and his lips were taut. He pressed his forehead to hers as they fought for footing in this strange and consuming dance.

"You're going to make me lose it, love. And I won't. Not here, not ever. You deserve so much more."

She tugged his shirt from his jeans. "I deserve you, and I want you."

"Vivian."

"Yes. That's my answer. What was your question?"

He growled.

His next kiss branded her soul as his.

Because tonight was the beginning.

The beginning of the end.

# Chapter 18

The plan was simple.

There was no plan.

Draven rubbed a hand slowly over his face as he stared at Clark's house and the multiple shadows within. The lights were dimmed, most likely for the sake of pleasing Garrett and his henchmen.

He had no idea the fury he'd walk into, and did his best to hide his uncertainty behind false calm. Garrett didn't like to wait and expected to be obeyed. He had wanted to speak the night after their last meeting, but Crazy paid Draven and Vivian a visit.

Three days later on Earth—he wasn't sure how long they had remained in the Celestial realm, since there was no cycle of day and night, not to mention he had been a *little* busy—and he was certain he'd get shot up with icy gazes the moment he walked through Clark's door.

He'd handle it.

What he struggled to hide was his disapproval with Vivian's instance on coming inside, too. And Kalen. To his great relief, Kalen had convinced Fawn to remain with Jackson and Sophia at the young scientist's house. At least that was something.

He glanced at Vivian. Gods, why wouldn't she agree to stay behind, too, to stay safe?

*You're supposed to die and she thinks she can save you.*

The truth didn't escape him, nor did it make him feel any better about tonight. Nalia said Cerryan would be handled by the High Guards after his direct attempt to confiscate Kalen's crown. But interfering with the vampires on Earth could be catastrophic.

Vivian had begged for other outcomes, but Nalia had refused to give in to her pleas.

Which meant he was probably about to walk into the hands of his executioner. Who wanted to plan their own death? Certainly not him, and he wouldn't set a plan in motion. Better to have his fate left up in the air if he had any chance of walking away from tonight to enjoy eternity with Vivian.

Oh, what he'd do to return to that glass room and gaze out at the universe with Vivian tucked beside him in bed.

*My sweet Vivian.*

She sat in the backseat and stared through the tinted windows of Kalen's sports scar. Her body was rigid, her chest barely moving from her lack of breathing and the deadly pace of her heart. Beside him, Kalen portrayed the epitome of a man of calm, seated back in the driver's seat, but his eyes were dagger sharp. A man not to be taken at face value.

"You said they are unaware of what we are," Kalen said quietly, breaking the dense silence. "It may benefit us until we know what we'll be dealing with."

"Walking corpses, Kalen. They're pathetic," Draven grumbled. "Abominations."

"They are vampire Elders and obviously powerful."

"We are young by their standards and full of vitality."

Kalen flicked his hand in a "so-you-say" motion that needled Draven's already tense nerves.

"Well, now's as good a time as any." Draven pushed open the passenger side door and stretched up onto his feet. Kalen appeared beside him. He suppressed his urge to slam the back door shut the moment he heard it open. Instead, he braced one hand on the door, one on the roof of the car, and leaned down to block Vivian from getting out. Her eyes were glazed over, her emotions unreadable. She wore the mien of a soulless creature, and Draven hated it. "I'm serious when I say you should consider staying in the car."

The corner of her mouth twitched.

Then she vanished.

Draven closed his eyes and gritted his teeth before he quietly closed the door and turned back to Kalen. The other man's expression failed to hide the degree of his distaste for his sister's stubbornness.

Vivian reappeared at her brother's side. She tilted her head and lifted a brow. "Ready?"

"No. Not until you agree to go back to Jackson's house," Draven said harshly, though he kept the volume low. He wouldn't put it past the bags of bones to hear them, even at this distance. "Fawn stayed behind, and for good reason."

Kalen grunted, muttering something in the Celestial tongue under his breath.

Vivian held out her hand for Draven to take. "I'm holding onto hope for tonight."

"With no weapons or backup." Draven groaned, capturing her hand and lifting her knuckles to nuzzle against his cheek for a brief moment.

"Nothing is set in stone, Draven. Prophecies are only as powerful as you allow them to become. If I have learned anything through my life, it is that we determine our own destinies, regardless of who and what tries to break us down along the way."

Draven stared at her for a long moment. Yeah, she yanked his heart from his chest and claimed him as her own. He was fine with it. It didn't take much to realize he had crashed and burned hard for his princess and goddess the night he bumped into her at Howler's.

"Well, then, let's write out our future, shall we?"

Draven tried to ignore the prickling foreboding along his neck as he led Vivian and Kalen up the driveway and to the front door. He paused only to release Vivian's hand—not because he wanted to, but for her own safety—before he unlocked the door and entered the house with all of his cocky confidence set in place.

If Death came calling tonight, he wasn't going down a coward.

Ice scraped along his mind. He turned to the living room.

"It's about time!"

Clark rushed to him from the hallway, drawing his attention from the living room before he spotted the source of the chill. His friend's eager concern washed away the moment his eyes found Vivian and Kalen. His mouth tightened and his shoulders grew stiff. He flashed a shaded glance toward the living room. The silence that stretched between them was fraught with question.

Draven merely nodded once, confirming his friend's unspoken question.

"Let me get you a beer. Anything for you two?" Clark asked, skillfully leaving out introductions.

"I think we're all okay for the moment." Draven broke Clark's gaze and moved toward the living room. The sight of the three Elders sitting on the sofa like Grim Reapers without their scythes would have been humorous if that didn't flush his prognosis for eternal life down the toilet. "Wasn't expecting a welcoming party."

Garrett's lips pulled back from his teeth. His obsidian eyes were nothing shy of Arctic cold, and they chilled Draven with poignant frustration.

"It is kind of you to arrive." Garrett's focus shifted to Vivian and Kalen. "With guests."

"Friends I've made the last few nights," Draven said. "I haven't kept you waiting, have I? Not that a few nights puts much of a dent in your aging process."

"You were nowhere to be found the last three nights." The coven leader's nostrils flared. "You waste our time when the matter at hand takes precedence." Garrett narrowed his eyes on Vivian. "To…frolic with an inconsequential woman?"

The second Draven saw Vivian's shoulders go rigid and her expression turn mulish, he mentally cursed. She'd experienced far too much pain and suffering in her life to let Garrett toss insults at her without repercussion. That much he knew.

However, now was not the time for power struggles.

He *really* wished Vivian had stayed with Fawn.

"Why are these creatures here?" Disgust dripped off Garrett's tongue like tar. "Their station is obviously below us. What are they?"

Draven and Kalen both gripped one of Vivian's shoulders as she opened her mouth, most likely to incriminate her identity. Draven had been very clear on the way over not to say a word about what breed of fae they were or the fact they were Sal's children. Vampire politics could be a tricky dance. The Levoire coven's politics were downright dirty.

"What do you suppose they are?" Draven asked, unable to keep the sharp edge from his tone. "You have plenty of old tomes in the library that would permit you to recognize their race."

"You would allow the female to speak her mind at will," Sylvester said with a sour edge. "Had you not restrained her."

"That's how things roll in this world, Sylvie," Draven mocked.

Garrett lifted a bony hand to silence both Brodan and Sylvester before they could retort. When his cronies subsided, he stood up and glided toward Vivian and Kalen. Draven and Kalen moved as one, pulling Vivian behind the wall of their bodies. At least his stubborn angel remained where they put her.

Kalen lifted his chin beneath Garrett's assessment, but remained silent. After a long moment, Garrett turned to Draven, disappointment roiling in his eyes.

"I expected more from you, Draven. Instead, you lower yourself to consort with mix-breeds."

Draven recognized the lethal purr of Garrett's voice.

So did Clark, who tried to wedge himself between Garrett and Draven. Faster than a snake, Garrett grabbed him by the throat and pitched him across the room. Clark slammed into the wall, leaving an impression of his body in the drywall that webbed and crumbled around him.

Brodan appeared at Clark's side, brandishing a short sword. Instead of metal, the blade was wood, tipped with silver, poised to pierce Clark through the chest. The threat was clear.

A calm, dangerous rage pulsed in Draven's mind. He had to keep himself in check or he'd see Clark turn into a mummy before disintegrating into ash.

Garrett's eyes narrowed on Kalen. "You certainly have your father's defiance in your eyes. A rather admirable quality when it isn't implemented foolishly."

Kalen's lips curled in a soundless snarl. A tick touched his cheek.

Garrett slid his piercing gaze to Draven, his grin far from friendly. "You did not think I would recognize who they were the moment I saw them, did you?" His brows rose. "Oh. You did."

Draven had no time to react before Sylvester yanked Vivian away and threatened her heart with a similar wooden short sword. The storm of fear and fury that laced her eyes was palpable. It resonated in his chest. He observed every detail of Sylvester's grip on her, mentally calculating how he would free her without harm.

As if to answer with a stern "you won't," Sylvester drew a bead of blood from the curve of her breast with the tip of the stake. Darkness cascaded over Vivian's expression, and her bared teeth silently screamed resistance.

"Your behavior toward them is quite concerning, Draven," Garrett continued.

A bark of pain caused Draven to jerk around in time to see Brodan step back from his handiwork. He'd pinned Clark to the ruined wall with a stake through his chest. Blood soaked the front of Clark's shirt, agony twisting his features. The stake missed his most vital organ, but rendered him helpless.

*What have you laced your medieval device with?*

"You've *befriended* them." The brittle words brought Draven's fury back to Garrett. He wasn't shocked to see Kalen facing the point of yet another stake, wielded by the leader himself. Kalen looked ready to tear the vampire's head off as he pressed back into the wall Garrett had pushed him to. "You've befriended our enemies."

Draven laughed, the sound lacking all humor. Rage dripped off his tongue. "Sal would be rolling over in his ash pile about now if he heard your rather poor opinion of his children, considering you're the one holding stakes to their chests."

Searing hot pain exploded through his gut as his body jolted forward. The hand that appeared on his shoulder and the nails that stabbed through his skin and muscle held him from falling to his knees. Brodan. Vivian's horrified scream pulsed in time with the waves of pain assaulting his body. His head dropped and he stared at the bloody tip of a stake protruding from his abdomen. Warmth oozed down his stomach and soaked into his shirt and the waistband of his jeans.

"Draven Lourdes, I will give you one opportunity to redeem yourself. Should you fail, you shall be sacrificed, and so shall your sister. Your rebellious ways have been tolerated long enough."

From the corner of his eyes, through the sheet of ebbing and flowing red in his vision, Vivian struggled in Sylvester's hold. Her eyes glowed, fear permeating her expression, caused by all the pain he suffered.

He had never hated the way he hated now. Hated the leader of the vampire coven who forced him to choose because now, he knew, Garrett was aware of his connection to Vivian. Malice shimmered in his evil gaze.

"It was brought to my attention by an unlikely source," Garrett stated. Kalen shifted against the wall and earned himself half an inch of the stake's tip in his chest. The man hissed, fists balled at his sides. "I still do not know who exactly came to our aid, but you have crossed a forbidden line with that despicable creature."

Vivian.

He roared as another stake pierced through his midsection, this time his lower back. It severed his spine and his legs went numb. The grip on his shoulder tightened, his bones stressed beneath the force of a vampire's strength keeping him from falling to the ground.

Throb. Throb. Throb.

He could barely see through the tide of red. The scent of his blood sent a chill down his arms.

"Let him go!" Vivian begged.

"Vivi," Kalen hissed.

"He is a *traitor*," Garrett seethed. "Naïve youth with no boundaries. No laws. No guidance. No hope."

Brodan drove Garrett's point home with yet another stake through Draven's midsection.

Draven grappled to hold onto consciousness. He knew if he gave into the blackness riding the waves of agony, he would never wake up.

He would never see his beautiful princess again.

The prophecy would be fulfilled, and he would die.

"So, Draven. Beg me for forgiveness," Garrett demanded. "Order their deaths and you will be saved."

Draven spit out the blood that bubbled up from his throat. He lifted his head and met Garrett's expectant gaze with every ounce of hate he could muster.

"Go to hell," Draven snapped, his voice wet with blood.

Garrett scowled.

Pain exploded from his chest. Light flashed behind his eyelids. The room disappeared.

And all went dark.

Agony ripped through her chest on iron claws and squeezed the life from her soul.

A scream tore up her throat and filled the house with bone-shattering grief.

Her grief.

The razor-sharp point of the stake digging mercilessly into her skin jerked away as a flurry of activity seized the electric air. Shouts. Commands. Sheriff Merrow's booming voice. Guns. Footsteps pounding around her. Flashes of shocking bright light.

All a blur as the vision of one of the vampires delivering a fatal blow to Draven branded her mind.

She dropped to the floor beside Draven and gathered his cold body into hers. Blood stained her trembling hands as she tried to stanch the bleeding. Splitters of wood stabbed at her fingers as her mind spun with questions. What could she do? How could she reverse this? Draven couldn't die. Not like this. Not *now*.

Strong yet tender hands landed on her shoulders. A sense of urgency slammed into her back.

"Vivi, we must go. Now," Kalen said quietly, his voice taut.

"I can't leave him." She choked. The frightening numbness that fell over her buckled when she spoke.

Kalen tugged her shoulders. "Now, Vivi."

"No," she moaned.

Kalen growled. She went airborne a moment later, her body bouncing as her belly folded over Kalen's shoulder.

He whisked her out of the house as she kicked and thrashed and punched at his back. She screamed into the night.

No sooner had they reached Kalen's car than a blast of gold- and blue-laced light blew out the windows of the house in a cacophony of shattering noise and soul-splitting shrieks.

Kalen dropped Vivian to her feet, gathered her close, and held her tightly in his embrace, his back to the house. Shards of glass plinked across the pavement around them and bounced off their clothes.

An eerie calmed settled over the night. Kalen loosened his hold on her to glance over his shoulder. Vivian braced herself for her worst nightmare.

Finality.

Sheriff Merrow had the three vampires cuffed and was leading them down to the numerous patrol cars blocking the road as they fought the werewolves holding them. Another officer aided Draven's vampire friend across the yard, the stake no longer embedded in his chest.

Hugh stalked out of the house with a middle-aged woman beside him. The woman was a stranger to Vivian. She walked with purpose and confidence, or maybe it was severity. Either way, the woman's being pulsed with unseen power. She held a wooden box between her hands.

When the woman swung her gaze to Kalen and Vivian, the sternness of her expression softened.

Hugh murmured something to the woman before leading her toward Kalen's car. Vivian stiffened as they approached.

"You shouldn't have to worry about them again," Hugh said, stopping to stand beside them. He motioned to the woman. "This is Alice Bishop. She's the coven leader for the local witches, and one of the most powerful witches I've ever known. Fawn tipped me off late last night and I asked Alice for her help."

Vivian glanced at the box in Alice's hands.

"Their powers. They possess no more strength or power than a human now, and will live eternally in this state."

"It's a brutal punishment for the undead," Hugh assured them.

Vivian stared. She listened to the words, but they didn't register. Cold. Numb. That's all she knew. Her legs moved, pulled by their own accord. Kalen's hands slid away from her, releasing her to the inevitable. The night faded at her back, leaving nothing more than a shell of herself to move silently up the glass-dotted yard to the equally silent house.

It wasn't until she stood in the spot she had last held Draven that she fell to her knees. Dead. That's how she felt. Dead. Like her charming soul mate.

She drew her hands through the wisps of what remained of Draven. Ribbons of ash and the weapons that stole him from her life.

Dead.

Along with any flickering spark of hope.

# Chapter 19

*One week later*

"Don't you look magnificent!" Delaney greeted them in the entryway into the ballroom. Vivian accepted her hug and a friendly kiss on the cheek before stepping aside so Fawn could receive a similar greeting. She looked around the ballroom, distantly fascinated by the degree of elegance in the decorations. Since losing Draven, nothing really touched her.

Pumpkins, hay, dozens upon dozens of exuberant and exotic floral bouquets. Tables lined with black and orange linens. Candlelight dancing over crystal and diamonds. The tiers of hors d'oeuvres and the spreads of fancy catered platters tempted her taste buds.

It was apparent not a cent had been spared on details, decorations, or the food. The ballroom was filled with Fawn's closes friends from Nocturne Falls. Friends who waved or approached with warm greetings.

Not a single friend could hide the glint of sympathy for Vivian behind their smiles and beaming expressions.

She would have stayed home had Fawn and Kalen not insisted she join them. She did so, against her better judgment. She didn't have the energy to argue. The wound to her heart was too raw, her pain too strong. At any moment, she feared she'd break down in tears.

One week. One week since Draven was killed.

One week since her hope threatened to abandon her. Only Nalia's words fed her the strength to grapple for the tattered ends of that hope. If she were bound to a life of suffering to deliver hope to others, then she would find some happiness in her pain.

*Such a twisted way of thinking.*

Hugh approached with Sheriff Merrow and his wife, Ivy. He graced her with a gentle hug. Ivy's embrace made up for the lack of fierceness in Hugh's. Vivian had to fight back the tears that sprang to her eyes.

"It's wonderful to see you here, Vivi. And you look marvelous. That blue dress was made for you," Ivy said quietly, close to her ear. She leaned back and smiled sadly. "Gorgeous, as always."

Vivian nodded. It was all she could do not to break out in sobs.

"I thought Jackson was coming," Hugh said to Fawn.

"He's fumbling around at home. He'll be here soon," Fawn assured. "He's bringing a date."

Hugh's brows rose. "A date? Well, this should be an interesting night, then."

Vivian turned toward the entrance when she heard a familiar voice. As if summoned, Jackson appeared in the doorway, rosy cheeked and nervously playing with the jacket hem of his black tux. She felt an involuntary pull of her lips when her focus shifted to Sophia standing beside him, dressed in a beautiful black and orange gown. She was a sight to behold with her pale skin, raven-black hair, and blue eyes. Eyes that hung on Jackson with admiration. Her time in the Celestial world had provided her with a temporary healing of her artificial light ailment.

*Just as the exchange between Draven and I cured me of the darkness, only to leave me desolate.*

Her throat knotted. She turned away, ashamed that she couldn't bear the sight of Sophia. The young woman resembled Draven far too much for Vivian's spirit to process.

"I'm going to grab some punch," Vivian said to Kalen, heading to the drink table before he could question her.

The night wore on, and so did the grief, scraping away at the facade she set in place. Only a handful of their friends knew the significance of Draven's loss, providing a bit of an odd reprieve. She couldn't bear it if everyone in attendance pitied her. She declined a few offers to dance, including one from her brother. She tried to placate his worry by forcing down something called caviar, and force she had to do. It tasted terrible, and she doubted it had anything to do with her churning stomach and lack of appetite.

This was turning into a torture worse than anything she suffered at the lab.

The dinner bell rang, signaling the formal sit-down meal.

There was no way she would suffer through more food, more talk, and more feigned happiness.

"Kalen," she said quietly after locating her brother in the crowd. He turned to her, his gaze warm. "I'm going to leave. I'm tired."

He drew his fingers down her cheek in his normal brotherly fashion. "Are you certain?"

She caught his hand and kissed his fingertips. "I am. You and Fawn enjoy the rest of the evening and I'll talk to you tomorrow." She nodded toward Jackson and Sophia. "They're really cute together."

Kalen didn't say a word, only kissed her forehead and watched her leave. She waited for her coat in the entryway as guests moved around her, coming and going. The valet arrived with the garment. She thanked him and gave him a tip, then headed toward the front door.

"Let me help you with that."

Vivian ignored the offer, and the familiarity of the voice. Her mind had been merciless in its tricks the last week.

"It's cold outside."

Vivian let out an exasperated breath and glanced over her shoulder in the direction of the phantom voice.

Her heart stopped.

The image of Draven dressed in a tux glided toward her in a manner that mimicked his grace and agility all too well.

She looked away and squeezed her eyes shut against the rush of hope and tears.

*Cruel, cruel joke.*

She hustled toward the door.

The torturous vision of Draven appeared in front of her, catching her arm in a tender grip that sent a flood of tingling heat over her skin.

"I couldn't help but find myself captivated by the angel in the blue dress among all the black and orange. You stood out like a goddess."

The charm. Oh, sweet gods, the charm. And that grin. The spark in his eyes.

*The heat.*

He leaned close. "I hope you aren't here with anyone. I would love to ask for a dance, Miss…?"

Vivian's chin quivered as he drew a finger over her cheek. She couldn't find the words.

"You're dead," she whispered. Her voice cracked.

The phantom Draven's grin grew. He leaned closer still, until his lips touched her ear and rocked every doubt from her mind. "I should be dead, but you saved me, love."

She jerked back. "Draven?"

He fit one palm against her cheek, lifting her chin with the fingertips of his other. "I don't think this world could handle two of me."

"But...but..." The tears broke through the gate and trekked down her cheeks. Her world spun on an unnatural axis.

Draven drew her close, brushing his lips over her cheeks, capturing her tears with soft, airy kisses. There was nothing incorporeal about him. Nothing, from the hand on her cheek to the hard chest beneath her knuckles as she gripped the lapels of his jacket and held tight.

"Sweet, beautiful Vivian." He let out a fierce breath before drawing her against him. Oh, his delicious scent filled her nostrils, feeding her a dangerous promise that this was not a dream. Not a cruel creation of her grief-stricken imagination. "My precious love."

"How is this possible?"

*I will not collapse. I will not lose control.*

"I guess Nalia believes I'm worthy of being your soul mate. I woke up in the Celestial plane. She told me my survival, and your cure, had to do with our blood exchange. And her fondness of our bond." He sighed and nuzzled her neck. "You're my goddess, Vivian. You rule me in every way possible. Your fae blood is superior to any vampire blood. Essentially, my drinking from you kept me alive."

"You didn't die."

A powerful revelation.

When Vivian finally looked up into Draven's very real and alive and beautiful face, she laughed and threw her arms around his neck. He groaned, his arms tightening around her waist and lifting her feet from the ground.

In that instant of their reunion, she caught a faint shimmer of golden light out in the yard. The gleaming silhouette of a woman. Of Nalia.

Her aunt smiled, her form fluttering like a sheet in the breeze. Vivian mouthed, "Thank you" as the apparition faded into the night.

"You weren't planning on leaving the ball so early, were you? I hear this event is catered by one of the top chefs. Directly from France," Draven murmured as he nuzzled her hair. "Mmm. *J'ai faim, ma belle déese.*"

"I think I've tired of the ball." She leaned back and smiled at Draven. "But the night is still young. We're both dressed for a night out. And I believe there is much to be celebrated."

"Most certainly. I think I have the perfect place in mind."

"Oh yeah?"

Draven smiled mischievously. "Your brother isn't around to dissuade you from riding on the back of my new bike in a dress. What do you say?"

How could she pass up a ride on a bike, wrapped close to Draven?

Draven.

Alive.

Oh, and that kiss he shared before pulling her by the hand to the end of the driveway.

The night belonged to them beneath the shimmer of stars and glow of the waning moon. The chilly fall air couldn't penetrate the heat that flowed between them.

Nothing could dampen the thrill of the ride, the night, proof of miracles and the drive of hope.

Draven brought them to the overlook, where he parked the bike and cut the engine. Tonight, they were alone. No other cars. Only the glowing show of lights from far below and the promise of forever above.

Draven climbed off the bike and helped her gather the silk of her blue floor-length gown. He spun her beneath his arm as her toes touched down on the ground, then pulled her close and began leading her in a dance to an unknown song.

"It will take more than a few stakes through my skin to rid you of me, love. You've laid claim to me, and I won't ever leave you," Draven murmured, swaying her slowly. "All you have to do is say the word."

"And what word is that?"

His hand slipped low on her back. "Yes."

She looked at him, melting beneath his charming smile. Her heart sputtered. "What is your question?"

"Be mine, Vivian Hawkins. Forever and ever. Say you'll be my everything. My wife, my queen, my goddess." His smile faded beneath the sincerity in his words. "My breath. My blood. My life."

She didn't want tears, but the ones that stung her eyes now were those of fulfillment. "Yes, my charming vampire. Yes, yes, and yes until I can say it no more." She pushed up on her toes, tipped her head and let her lips linger on his. "I love you, Draven Lourdes. I love everything about you. Just don't you *ever* almost die on me again."

He chuckled. "I don't plan on it. I have no intention of leaving the only woman I will ever love."

And he sealed that promise with a deep kiss that filled her with all the hope the universe could offer.

The End

# About Kira Nyte

Born and raised a Jersey girl with easy access to NYC, I was never short on ideas for stories. I started writing when I was 11, and my passion for creating worlds exploded from that point on. Romance writing came later, since kissing gave you cooties at 11, but when it did, I embraced it. Since then, all of my heroes and heroines find their happily ever after, even if it takes a good fight, or ten, to get there.

I currently live in Central Florida with my husband, our four children, two bunnies, two hermit crabs, parakeet and fish. I work part-time as a PCU nurse when I'm not writing or traveling between sports and other activities.

I love to hear from readers!
Contact me at kiranyteauthor@gmail.com

27791037R00115

Made in the USA
Middletown, DE
20 December 2018